Lilly The Plain One.
Lilly The Brain.

Lilly, who had far too much pragmatism to court
dreams of wonder. And here she was, tormenting
herself with the touch and smell and sound of the
very kind of man she'd built those walls to protect
herself against.

Pretty girls could expect to see an answering
spark in the eyes of a man like Ethan. Lovely
women with deep, melting eyes and the kind of
figure that seemed poured over a perfect frame
and set to movement with the wind.

Lilly hadn't been poured. She'd been built.

Thank heavens his eyes were closed again.
That way he couldn't see the tears that wouldn't
dissipate. This was so stupid, Lilly thought. She
knew better. She'd known so much better her
whole life that she'd structured everything so
she wouldn't even be tempted.

Tempted to fall in love with a man she could
never have....

Dear Reader,

Hey, look us over—our brand-new cover makes Silhouette Desire look more desirable than ever! And between the covers we're continuing to offer those powerful, passionate and provocative love stories featuring rugged heroes and spirited heroines.

Mary Lynn Baxter returns to Desire and locates our November MAN OF THE MONTH in the *Heart of Texas,* where a virgin heroine is wary of involvement with a younger man.

More heart-pounding excitement can be found in the next installment of the Desire miniseries TEXAS CATTLEMAN'S CLUB with *Secret Agent Dad* by Metsy Hingle. Undercover agent Blake Hunt loses his memory but gains adorable twin babies—and the heart of lovely widow Josie Walters!

Ever-popular Dixie Browning presents a romance in which opposites attract in *The Bride-in-Law.* Elizabeth Bevarly offers you *A Doctor in Her Stocking,* another entertaining story in her miniseries FROM HERE TO MATERNITY. *The Daddy Search* is Shawna Delacorte's story of a woman's search for the man she believes fathered her late sister's child. And a hero and heroine are in jeopardy on an island paradise in Kathleen Korbel's *Sail Away.*

Each and every month, Silhouette Desire offers you six exhilarating journeys into the seductive world of romance. So make a commitment to sensual love and treat yourself to all six!

Enjoy!

Joan Marlow Golan
Senior Editor, Silhouette Desire

Please address questions and book requests to:
Silhouette Reader Service
U.S.: 3010 Walden Ave., P.O. Box 1325, Buffalo, NY 14269
Canadian: P.O. Box 609, Fort Erie, Ont. L2A 5X3

Sail Away
KATHLEEN KORBEL

Published by Silhouette Books
America's Publisher of Contemporary Romance

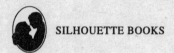 SILHOUETTE BOOKS

ISBN 0-373-76254-2

SAIL AWAY

Copyright © 1999 by Eileen Dreyer

KATHLEEN KORBEL

lives in St. Louis with her husband and two children. She devotes her time to enjoying her family, writing, avoiding anyone who tries to explain the intricacies of the computer and searching for the fabled housecleaning fairies. She's had her best luck with her writing—from which she's garnered a *Romantic Times Magazine* award for Best New Category Author of 1987, the 1990 Romance Writers of America RITA Award for Best Romantic Suspense and the 1990 and 1992 RITA Awards for Best Long Category Romance—and with her family, without whom she couldn't have managed any of the rest. She hasn't given up on those fairies, though.

To Jill Marie Landis, *Mahalo nui*
And to Ethan.
Thanks for going through all this
to make me feel better.

Prologue

Noah Campbell was ready for a hot bath. He'd just spent the past four days convincing a large herd of cattle that they really did want to head up to higher pastures, and he was exhausted. He was also filthy, bruised, battered, and happy as hell to be home.

"This sure ain't Hollywood, is it, boss?" his foreman asked as they guided their weary mounts across the Bitter River.

Lifting his hat to wipe the sweat from his forehead, Noah grinned like a kid. "Thank God for small favors."

Not that Noah minded his other job in Hollywood. After all, being the world's number-one box-office draw under the name of Cameron Ross provided him with the cash to run his ranch the way he wanted. Heck, it had provided him with the ranch in the first place. But it also made it tough to escape to his real home without hordes of paparazzi trailing him.

To that end, he'd sent his cousin Ethan in the opposite direction the way he always did, so the press, long since taught to see the movie star Cameron Ross in Ethan Campbell's similarly rugged features, would follow and record. Noah, slouched in his saddle with a four-day growth of beard and an urgent need of a bath, could relax.

"When you due back?" Hank asked.

"Beginning of next week. After I take Dulcy to the doctor's."

Dulcy. His wife of eight months, who was even now eight months pregnant, tied to the house and testy as a mare with a burr under her saddle. Until the last month, Dulcy had run the ranch single-handed. She still wasn't happy about not being allowed to join in the drive, but the doctor had been adamant. Whether Dulcy liked it or not, neither her physician nor her husband was going to let her wrangle cattle up in the high mountain meadows when she could barely fit in her saddle.

Which was why Noah wasn't surprised to see her standing out in the yard waiting for him to show up. Tiny, redheaded, round as a watermelon. Hand to eyes to shade them against the setting sun. Noah waved and kicked his gelding into a canter. Dulcy waved back, something in her hand, and began walking forward.

Walking fast, her movements taut and aggressive.

Noah hadn't been married long, but he'd been married long enough to know what that posture meant. Something was wrong. Without even realizing it, he nudged his horse into a dead run.

"What's the matter?" he asked as he skidded to a stop and swung down.

Dulcy had a death's grip on a newspaper. Her face was screwed up in worry, and her hand was at her belly.

Noah grabbed her. "Dulcy? What is it?"

She handed over the paper. "We were just headed up to find you," she said. "I think you'd better read this."

Noah didn't have to read more than the headlines. "Oh, God. I have to go."

"*We* have to go," she said simply.

He took one look at the tight cast of her eyes and knew it wouldn't do any good to argue. His chest was on fire, and he'd just found out. She must have been chewing on this thing for twelve hours or more. "We'll go," he said, and curled an arm around her shoulder to support her. She wouldn't have it, though. She just wrapped her arms around his neck and held him and didn't ask what else this would mean, even though they both knew.

They didn't care. It didn't matter that the headline meant his anonymity was over, his cover blown like a storm door in a twister. It didn't matter that their island of domestic normalcy would never be recovered. What mattered was why.

Noah wouldn't remember dropping the newspaper. He just held on to his wife, suddenly terrified to his very soul. On the ground, the breeze riffled at the pages, but the headline on the front page was too big to miss. Just above the picture of Noah in his tux at the Academy Awards, screamed the words: Cameron Ross Missing and Feared Dead Off Hawaiian Islands.

One

He wasn't missing, really. Just seriously misplaced. At least, he thought he must be, since he couldn't remember how he'd gotten here. Or why. Or when. All he knew was that he was lying on his back in the water looking up at a very blue, very bright sky. And that his head hurt. And his leg. And his ribs on his right side. Other than that, he figured he was probably just fine.

He tried to sit up, but that just made his head hurt worse. He closed his eyes, but that didn't seem to help. He was thirsty, he was dizzy and he was a little seasick.

He was late. He knew that. He was supposed to be somewhere. He was supposed to be doing something. Something important. But whatever it was refused to be identified. And, truthfully, he didn't try hard. It was too much effort. He should probably just stick to finding out where he was.

The raft. He should look at the raft he was lying on.

Maybe he could find some kind of clue, a boat's name or return address or something. He opened his eyes.

No clue. Just a big white inflatable raft with nothing in it but him…in a tuxedo. With bare feet. And a big black Stetson lying across his stomach. In the middle of miles and miles of water.

That settled it. The only thing he managed to do with his eyes open was confuse himself. He closed them and kept them closed. And then, just for extra measure, he plopped the hat over his eyes to keep out the sun.

He really wasn't sure how long he'd been drifting. Minutes. Hours. Days. He was sweating, and he could tell his neck and hands were burning in the hot tropical sun, but he couldn't seem to manage the energy to move. The drift of the water beneath him was just too soothing, the breeze only strong enough to cool the sweat on his chest. So he lay there like a well-dressed lump and let the sun cook him to the color of a rare roast and wondered where he was supposed to be.

"Hello? Can you hear me?"

He heard her. He ignored her. Probably a gorgeous woman in an evening dress to go with his tux.

The thought damn near made him laugh. This sun really was frying his brain.

"Hey! Are you all right?"

Her voice was closer now. Maybe she was a mermaid. Or a navy-trained dolphin who'd broken the language barrier. Unless she had his itinerary in her hand with full explanations, he really didn't want to know.

"Go away." He sounded like hell.

She laughed, an abrupt burst of surprise. "Why?" she asked, very near now, her voice like that of the Lorelei on the Rhine—except with a different accent. "You waiting for a date?"

He didn't bother to look over or remove his hat. He was dizzy enough as it was. "Sure seems to me like it's a definite possibility."

She laughed again, and he wanted to smile. "Well, I seriously doubt anybody's going to want to dance with you looking like that."

"Don't be silly," he told her. "I'm in my best clothes...at least, I think I am."

"You think?"

He shrugged. "I'm not sure of much right now...except that my head is killing me. You have any aspirin?"

"How 'bout if I take you in to land and we can find some?"

That was what finally got his eyes open. "Land? There's land?"

"Of course there's land. Where do you think I came from?"

"Twenty thousand leagues under the sea." He tilted the hat enough so he could squint in the direction of her voice. All he could make out was an expressionist painting of colors. Lurid yellows and oranges in overlapping triangles, the blue of the ocean, and a smaller series of shapes and colors that involved flickering black, deep tan and bright red, tilting and repeating themselves into a pattern that was somehow familiar, no matter how weird. He interpreted it as a shapely woman on a small sailboat, done by Picasso.

He shook his head. "Oh, no you don't," he demurred, dropping the hat back over his eyes. "Just let me bake in peace."

"That's exactly what you're going to do if you don't get off the water," she protested.

He felt a bump alongside the raft and tried to ignore it.

A mirage. A noisy mirage that smelled like coconut oil and plumeria.

"How do I know what plumeria smells like?" he wondered out loud.

Busy doing something that made the raft buck and sway, she ignored his question. "Come on, you need to get someplace safe. Can you tell me what happened?"

"I fell off a boat."

"I guessed that. What boat?"

He frowned in concentration. "Don't know."

That didn't seem to bother her. "Probably happened during the storm. You're lucky you ended up so close to land. Now, if you'll take off that hat and open your eyes, you need to help me get you over."

He sighed, unbelievably tired, even after just lying around for...for how long? He remembered darkness, the jolt of cold water. A struggle trying to get shiny black pumps off in the water. Which made just about as much sense as anything else he remembered.

"I don't suppose you could just tow me back like this?"

"Not in a sailboat," she assured him. "Besides, if you can get over here, I have water."

Water. That got his eyes open again. It got his limbs to move, although no one would have confused the results for anything graceful.

"God, I am thirsty," he admitted, only now realizing how very hoarse his voice was. His throat was as charred as his face. He got all the way up, dizzy as hell, and almost landed in the water in his first attempt to get over into the sleek little sailboat.

"Oh, man," she breathed in surprise, even as she held on to his raft with one hand and held the other out for him. "Your face is all bloody. You took quite a whack."

He shook his head and almost ended up in the water all over again. He thought he was usually pretty nimble. He sure as hell wasn't now. "I sure hurt like I did."

He'd just about managed to lean forward into her boat when suddenly she just let go. "Oh, my God..." she whispered as the boats bumped and skipped away from each other. "You're..."

This time he got a mouthful of water before she pulled him up.

"I do something...wrong?" he sputtered.

She was frozen solid, as if she'd just seen him rise from the dead. "You're Cameron Ross!" she squeaked, almost letting go of the boat again.

He blinked at her. "You know who I am?"

She laughed, that musical, sweet sound that seemed to skip across the water. "You're kidding, right? Who doesn't know who you are?"

He frowned a moment. Took a look down at the bloodstains on what had probably once been a snowy tux shirt. Looked back up to what he figured was probably a very pretty young woman who held on to his arm as if he was about to splinter to pieces. Did his best to smile.

"Me."

All Lilly had been looking forward to this afternoon was a few last hours of peace and quiet. A slow sail home from the old cabin on Molokai, where she'd been taking a few days away from the family. From the job. From the claustrophobia of Oahu, where too many people made too much noise and she was forced to participate.

Today she'd meant to have wind and water and sky. She'd ended up with Cameron Ross instead.

"Come on," she urged him, trying her best to sound

pragmatic and purposeful when she just wanted to shake. She wanted, ridiculously enough, to giggle.

He was beautiful. Every bit as rugged and dashing as he was said to be, with that just-too-long dark hair and those crystal-blue eyes. Dimpled chin, perfect nose and broad chest. And all of that floating in a life raft in a tux and Stetson. Who said life was mundane?

He didn't look *exactly* like himself, Lilly decided, but that didn't matter. Her cousin Koki, who had worked on *Magnum, P.I.,* assured her that nobody really looked just like they did on screen. Cameron Ross looked good enough, that was for sure. Good enough to give Lilly weak knees.

Which wasn't going to be much help, when he was hurt and confused and lost out in the Pacific on a life raft. So Lilly swallowed her surprise and reached out, not to Cameron Ross, but to the injured man in the life raft.

"Here," she coaxed. "You get over here, and we'll get some water in you. You really got smacked on the head. That's probably why you don't remember. Soon as I get you ashore, we can take a look at it. Are you dizzy or anything?"

"I'm dizzy and everything," he assured her, his voice gravelly and tired.

She took hold of solid, strong arms and leaned back until his face was almost in her neck so he could get his legs over. He really must have been hurt. She'd seen Cameron Ross dance through a fight scene like Baryshnikov. Now he could hardly move four limbs at once.

And then she saw more blood.

"What did you do to your leg?" she asked, trying her darnedest not to inhale the earthy smell of him. The sharp tang of sweat, the darker, smokier hint of cologne. It was distracting her from the rusty stain just above his left knee.

He flopped over into her little boat and took a distracted look down at his leg, as if somebody had left him with one he hadn't used before. "I don't know...hurts, though."

"Can you sit up?" Lilly asked. "Just for a minute. You need to get that jacket off."

It took some struggling and more than one surprised grunt of pain, but between them they managed, while Lilly held her breath and tried valiantly to ignore the spread of his shoulders and the curl of chest hair that glistened beneath an unbuttoned collar.

Then, settling him back on the deck, she reacquainted him with his hat and broke out the bottled water she always carried with her. "It's not cold," she offered. "But it's wet."

He just lay there at her knees, his eyes closed. The skin around his eyes and mouth was white, in contrast with the raw red of the rest of his face. His chest rose and fell in short, ragged breaths. His eyes were closed and his mouth open. Lilly tried not to be afraid. Her first movie star, and he was going to die on her boat because she'd taken off his jacket.

"Mr. Ross?" she whispered, a hand out to his head. Almost. She couldn't quite touch him, as if her intentions and her fantasies were getting scrambled.

He didn't answer. Just lay there, breathing with a funny grunting sound Lilly recognized all too well. She had three very large brothers who played sports and loved nothing more than a good fight. Unless Lilly had wasted all that time in emergency rooms, Mr. Ross had hurt his chest. Or worse.

"Mr. Ross, please," she begged, now touching him. Feathering her fingers against his hair, along his cheek, his throat. Just to make contact, to reassure herself with his warmth. "Please. You need some water."

He gave another little grunt and then startled awake, flinching. "Sorry...I, uh...don't feel very...good."

She tried smiling upside down into fabulous robin's-egg-blue eyes that were now clouded and tight. "You have every right not to. Take some water and then put your hat back over your head so I can get us to Maui."

He blinked at her. "Maui? Is that where I was going?"

She gave up waiting for him to lift his head and did it for him, resting it against her thighs so he could drink. "That's not even where *I* was going. I was on my way back to Oahu, but we're much closer to Maui, and I think you need closer. Now, drink."

He did, gulping, so the water ran down his neck. He raised his hands to cup hers and closed his eyes. Lilly let him drink a little and then pulled it away. "I have plenty," she assured him. "You need to take it easy."

He rested his head back against her thighs, still watching her. "Thank you. I think...I think you've just saved my sorry butt."

She couldn't help smiling again. "Trust me," she said. "It's my pleasure."

She even prided herself on not mentioning how very *not* sorry his butt was. His feet were bare, she suddenly realized. Now, why did that make her giddy? She wasn't exactly a foot fetishist, but the idea of bare feet on a man wearing a tux was unbelievably erotic. Besides, they were beautiful feet. Long and strong and graceful. But Lilly shouldn't have time to think of that either. She should have been thinking that they were probably going to blister from that sunburn.

She couldn't quite think that, though.

"Can I ask?" he asked. "How you know me?"

Lilly dragged her attention back to the look of uncertainty he was sharing with her. "Everyone in the civilized world knows you, Mr. Ross. You're probably the most famous movie star there is."

He stared at her for a minute, processing. Then he just snorted. "No, I'm not."

Lilly laughed. "Oh, I'm afraid you are."

"What about you?" he asked.

She should be moving. She couldn't manage it. Somehow, even battered and bloody, he had managed to dredge up the most delightful sparkle in those eyes of his. "What about me?" she asked, breathless all over again.

"Are you a movie star?"

"Almost," she said with a bright grin. "I'm a librarian."

Now he smiled. Really smiled. It was a softer smile than on screen, less assured. A little boy's smile, all heart and humor, and Lilly understood just why he'd earned that reputation he had as a lady-killer.

"And my name's Cameron Ross?" he said.

She nodded.

He thought about it for a second. "Doesn't sound right. I don't know why, but it..." He shook his head, closed his eyes. "There's something else, too. Something I think I should remember. And something I'm supposed to be doing...."

Lilly found herself perilously close to stroking his cheek again, just to soothe that look of tension. Instead, she straightened. "Well, it'll wait 'til we get you back in. Or at least to a motorboat that can get you there faster. If you'd had the good sense to fall off your boat on the south side of Molokai, you would have been picked up in a minute. It's lousy with traffic down there, and within sight of Maui and Lanai both. On this side there's just water."

"And you."

"And me. Who should have paid a lot more attention to her Tutu Mary when she was teaching me first aid."

"Tutu Mary? Who's that, a ballerina?"

If anybody else had asked that, Lilly would have bristled. Somehow Cameron Ross failed to make the old joke offensive.

"*Tutu* is Hawaiian for grandmother," Lilly explained. "My tutu was a healer. She tried to teach me, but I was better at theory than practice."

At least, that was what Lilly had always contended.

He smiled again. A soft smile of understanding. "I know first aid."

Lilly smiled back. "Of course you do."

Even so, she checked his leg to find that the bleeding was old, the tear in the slacks minimal. She checked his head to find a couple of good gashes up beyond the hairline, and one along his temple that some fancy plastic surgeon was probably going to charge a fortune to fix. Nothing was bleeding actively, though. Lilly couldn't see anything else obvious, and she couldn't do anything about it if she did, so she decided it was time to sail.

"Here," she said, wetting down a beach towel and draping it over his blood-caked head. "I'm going to give you your hat back to keep the sun out of your eyes."

She did, tilting it just enough that he could feel the wind underneath.

"Is that Molokai over there?" he asked, closing his eyes.

Lilly turned to see the undulating curtain of emerald cliffs that seemed to simply spill from the clouds straight into the glistening sea.

"It is," she said, her voice unconsciously softer.

"Can't believe I didn't notice it before. Can't we just go there?"

"Not on the north coast," she said. "No way to get you to civilization from there."

"It's beautiful."

Lilly smiled like a fond parent. "It is."

Actually, there was civilization on the north coast. Kalaupapa. A small peninsula of lush green that had been poured straight down the side of those forbidding cliffs to form a perfect tongue atop the sea. It held a community. It had medical care. Lilly had actually given brief thought to staying on her original course and landing there. But the only people living on the Kalaupapa peninsula were the last of Father Damien's children, elderly survivors of Hansen's Disease. Leprosy. As rigidly as they now guarded their privacy and shelter, Lilly wasn't sure they wanted the notoriety of a famous star dumped on their doorstep. Besides, Maui would be much better suited to transporting and pampering somebody who wore tuxes and sailed in yachts. Carefully climbing to her feet so she didn't disturb Cameron, Lilly untied the boom and set to work.

"I remember a storm," he said, his voice muffled as Lilly gently eased the little Sunfish over around the way she'd come. "Lots of noise and lights."

"Night before last," she said, gingerly stepping over him. "It was a beaut. I almost lost a roof and a radio in it. We're expecting a bigger one later. I was trying to get home before it got too close when I spotted you."

"I remember...diving. Diving? That's stupid. Why would I dive?"

"Probably falling off the side. Was it a sailboat?" she asked. "A cabin cruiser? Do you know if you had a crew?

If you were on a ship of any size, there's probably a search out for you.''

If she'd actually listened to that radio she'd had at the cabin, she might have known. But she'd walked. Thought. Wished.

Mr. Ross lifted a hand to rub gently at his chest. Sore, Lilly thought. There'd probably be a bruise or two under that once-starched tux shirt.

"I don't...remember,'' he admitted. "I don't remember much more than the wind and lightning, and trying like hell to get my shoes off. But I feel like...like there's something important I'm forgetting.''

"More important than your name?'' she asked, alternating her attention between him and her task. The wind had caught her sail, and the little boat skipped like a flat rock, the wind spinning her hair out behind her and cooling the sweat on her chest and back from the effort of hauling in a strange man.

"Not like name important,'' he said slowly, thinking hard beneath that hat. "But important.''

"Well, don't worry about it,'' Lilly said, much more blithely than she felt. "As soon as we get you ashore, you'll have plenty of time to remember.''

They were still quite a ways from help of any kind, but with any luck, once they swung into the Pailolo Channel they would run into a good-sized yacht, maybe a deep-sea fishing charter, that wouldn't mind conveying Mr. Ross to a doctor. And, if worse came to worst, Maui was only about five miles beyond.

Wait 'til she told her mother, Lilly thought with a stunned little shake of her head. Wait 'til she told her colleagues. *So there I was, minding my own business, just breaking the speed record between Molokai and Oahu, and who do I happen to rescue in his tux and Stetson but*

Cameron Ross? They wouldn't believe it. Heck, *she* still didn't believe it.

The brightly striped orange-and-yellow sail strained with the wind, and the cliffs of Molokai were slipping slowly past. Time to check her patient again. Lilly once again tied off the boom and bent to retrieve the water.

"Mr. Ross?" she asked.

He didn't answer. She panicked.

"Oh, please don't do this to me," she begged, dropping right back to her knees to shake his shoulder. "I'm not good in a crisis."

She lifted his hat to find him squinting up at her. "Doin' okay by me," he said with a rakish grin.

Lilly almost clobbered him. "Don't do that. I think you're not supposed to fall asleep, but I can't remember why. Health wasn't my section."

"Your section of what?"

"Research. I'm a research librarian. I can find the information once I get home, but I can't remember it. All I can remember is the line of Stuart succession."

He scowled. "Well, don't tell me that. I'd be out in a nanosecond."

Lilly wanted to smile. "Not into British royalty, huh?"

"Nope."

"How 'bout Hawaiian royalty? I can name you that succession, too."

"How about telling me your name? Since you seem to know mine."

"Lilly," she said, handing over the bottle of water. "Lilly Kokoa."

He squinted again. "Named after that Hawaiian queen? Liliuokailani?"

"Nope. The flower. I was born on Easter."

He grinned. "Not nearly as romantic. You are Hawaiian, aren't you?"

"Half. Quarter Portuguese, quarter Chinese. I'm a mutt."

He squinted again, as if assessing. "I'm no judge right now, but I'd bet that when I can actually see you, you'll be the best-looking mutt I've ever come across."

Lilly frowned down at him. "What do you mean, when you can see? Can't you see?"

His shrug was minimal. "It'll probably clear up. I'm already less sick."

Lilly knew he was trying to ease her mind. He wasn't having much success. Not only did she know perfectly well how she looked, she knew just what it meant that he couldn't tell. She'd lied to him about not knowing about head injuries. She knew enough, and he was scaring her again.

"Have some more water," she begged, hoping that maybe it was dehydration talking rather than head injury. After all, if he'd really fallen out of his boat the night before last, he'd been out in the sun an awfully long time.

"Thank you, Lilly," he agreed, once again wrapping his hands around hers to bring the bottle to his lips.

He had wonderful hands, she thought. Beautiful, long-fingered and callused from real work. Marred by nicks and old scars across a couple of knuckles. Strong hands. Lilly watched them, watched him sip the water, his eyes closed, the liquid dribbling down his throat. And she thought he didn't look a thing like a pampered movie star. His hands hadn't been manicured in a while, and his face was rough with old beard and new sunburn. Even in the tux, he looked like an outcast. A sexy, charismatic, vulnerable outcast.

And Lilly had been alone for too long, she decided, pulling away before her libido got the best of her.

"You don't want to rush that," she warned him, closing the bottle with hands that shook just a little. "It could make you sick."

"More research?" he asked, his voice weary and sore.

"No. Several viewings of *Man on the Run,* that movie you did where you were lost in the desert."

He got one eye open. "Uh huh."

"Come to think of it," she said with a grin, "you were in a tux there, too."

He sighed. "Must be my standard uniform for disasters."

Lilly was about to answer him when an air horn interrupted her. She whipped around to see an ocean-going yacht bearing down on them from the west.

"Now, how come I didn't see that?" she demanded, shading her eyes with her hand.

Cameron tried to look past her. "A boat?"

"More like a cruise ship."

Pulling out an emergency flare, she lit it and waved it over her head. The ship honked again and increased its speed until it was almost up to her little Sunfish. Lilly had to crane her neck to see up to the cabin.

"Do you need help?" a gravelly voice boomed through a megaphone.

"I have an injured man!" Lilly yelled through cupped hands. "Can you help me get him to a doctor?"

"Uh, wait…" Cameron protested, trying to sit up.

Lilly immediately pushed him back. "It's okay," she said. "They can move faster than I can."

"Happy to!" the other ship answered. "We'll pull alongside."

Cameron dropped the hat, squinting hard at the sleek

white yacht with its bristling aerials and gleaming brass. "There's something...I don't..."

"Mr. Ross, please," Lilly begged, a hand at each shoulder. "You're going to hurt yourself."

"No, I'm not," he argued, pushing her away with sudden strength and sitting up. "They are."

"What?" Lilly demanded.

"Hold it right there," the voice from the ship demanded.

Lilly spun around to find herself staring up into a double-barrelled shotgun. Alongside the man holding it stood two more people holding automatic weapons, each smiling as if they'd just found gold.

"Good to see you again, Mr. Ross," the guy with the shotgun greeted them. "I knew you wouldn't deliberately ruin a good kidnaping."

Lilly turned back to see that Cameron had gone very white. He turned toward her with a half-hearted smile. "I think I know what it is I needed to remember."

Two

Lilly was a blur. More to the point, everything was a blur. He wasn't sure why, but that didn't scare him the way it probably should have. Then again, that could have been simply because the guns were scaring him much, much more.

"I wish you hadn't gone and involved somebody else," his captor said to him with an odd sincerity. "I hate collateral damage."

Considering the fact that they'd just watched Lilly's bright little Sunfish being dispatched to the bottom of the ocean, he bet Lilly was wincing at that one.

"What a charming term," she said, posture erect and defiant. "You were with the military, weren't you?"

There was a smile in the guy's voice. "Yes, ma'am, I sure was."

"Until that little misunderstanding with the grenades and the CO's wife," one of the others piped up.

Captor number-one spun around. "That wasn't my fault."

They were all standing out on the deck of the yacht: three guys, Lilly and he in a tableau straight out of a movie. Between the smack on the head and the fact that every time he put weight on his left leg it just gave out on him, he was pretty much being held up by Lilly as the three guys—for some reason he thought of them as Huey, Duey and Louie—discussed the finer points of a good kidnaping. Which did not, Huey insisted, include collateral damage.

Huey was short, squat, with a sailor's rolling walk, and, from the shine on the top of his head, no hair to speak of. His voice sounded more like a big brother's than a big gangsta's, as if he were trying hard to break the other two in without help.

The other two were pretty much interchangeable to somebody with blurred and double vision. Tall, thin, brown, with shortish hair the color of Lilly's. So far only Duey had spoken. Louie kept quiet. And kept his gun pointed directly at Lilly's midsection.

Lilly.

God, he wished they would get whatever theatrics they had in mind over with so he could go back to laying his head in Lilly's lap. Forget yachts and movies and kidnapers. He wanted to lie back, close his eyes and just sink into the featherlight stroke of her fingers, the glitter of her laughter as it skipped over the water like sunlight.

Maybe it was the fact that he was still foggy and lost. Maybe it was the fact that she'd saved him. Or maybe it was the fact that she had a voice that could ease heartache and a lap that was as soft as a sigh, but he had a feeling he was going to get seriously stupid over her.

And he didn't even know what stupid was for him.

Startled at his own loss of focus, he shook his head. There was a gun pointed at Lilly's chest, and he was thinking about tropical breezes and puppy love. He needed to concentrate.

Unfortunately, all that shake had done for his head was to send it spinning again.

"We need to get going, boss," a new voice interrupted. "Let's get them below before Mister Moviestar just keels over."

He squinted hard at the third member of the kidnaping party. Time to reassess that first impression. He hadn't been kidnaped by Huey, Duey and Louie. He'd been kidnaped by Huey, Duey and *Louise*. Boy, did he wish he could remember what had happened!

"Tell you what," he offered as nonchalantly as he could. "Let the young lady go, and I'll be happy to fall down wherever you want me to."

"We just finished sinking her boat," Huey reminded him tersely.

"Isn't that the life raft I was in right behind you?"

Nobody turned. "We couldn't just leave it out there. People are already lookin' for you. And sooner or later somebody's gonna find your crew on that deserted island."

"Lilly can get to Molokai on the raft," he said. "Let her go. I'll cooperate if you let her go."

"No," Lilly argued.

"No," Huey, Duey *and* Louise echoed decisively.

He moved to argue with all four of them, but that just set off the dizziness again. Everything was suddenly tilting like a carnival ride. Damn, this wasn't working right.

"Mr. Ross is badly injured," Lilly said in that deceptively soft voice of hers as she tightened her hold on him. "You need to get him some help."

"Well, he wouldn't'a been hurt if he'd just stayed on board like a good boy," Louise retorted. "We would have had the ransom and dropped him off just like we promised by now."

"Ransom," he said, more to himself than anybody else. His head pounding and his stomach swirling, he turned his attention to Lilly, who, with both of them upright, only stood as tall as his armpit. "I guess that settles it. I must be Cameron Ross."

It still felt wrong. Fit wrong, like a badly tailored shirt, as if he'd pulled a name out of somebody else's closet. For some reason, he was sure it was something not to be discussed in front of Huey, Duey and Louise, however.

"You *guess?*" Duey demanded with an outraged snort. "What are your other choices—Beavis and Butthead?"

"Madonna," Huey added.

"Elvis," Louise retorted.

"Hey," Duey protested. "I seen Elvis. And he ain't no Elvis."

He was starting to sweat and sway. Not good. Lilly knew, though. Lilly tightened her grip. After a quick look in his direction that he thought might have been concern, she glared at their captors.

"What he *is,*" she said through gritted teeth, "is hurt. And if you don't let him lie down soon, he'll be dead before you can get any ransom. Is that what you had in mind?"

"You tellin' us what to do?" Duey demanded.

"Shut up," Huey snapped in his best military tone. "Get 'em locked back in. And don't you two do nothin' stupid in there."

"How stupid is vomiting?" he asked.

That got them to move fast.

* * *

"Better?" Lilly asked ten minutes later, her voice inches from his left ear.

He didn't bother to open his eyes. It was one thing to be dramatically injured in front of a beautiful woman. It was another to be ignominiously sick, especially when she had to hold your head while you did it.

"Yeah."

He felt a cool, wet cloth being draped over his forehead and thought he would die from the simple pleasure of it. The gentle attention of those butterfly hands.

"I think I'm in love," he managed.

She laughed. "You're not very choosy."

He smiled back, eyes still closed. "Any girl with a rag in a time of need."

She was quiet for a moment. Looking around, he imagined. He could hardly blame her. He was lying on a bed the size of Rhode Island in a room that looked more like a country house than a ship's cabin. Dark walnut paneling, lush green carpeting, recessed lighting and an entertainment center. Windows instead of portholes, and big vases of what had been fresh flowers a couple of days ago, though they now wilted at alarming angles. At least, that was what he assumed. As bad as his vision was, that could have been a bad wall sculpture of linoleum and shag he was trying to decipher.

"Well," Lilly said with a half sigh, "if you're going to be kidnaped, you might as well do it in style."

"My thoughts exactly."

"You don't sound particularly worried."

"I'm sure that once I remember what this is all about I'll be terrified. Right now I'm concentrating on not humiliating myself again."

Another instinctive flutter of fingers against his cheek. He wondered if she even realized she was doing that. She was a toucher, tactile contact as much a part of her communication as words and expressions. He wasn't sure, but he didn't think he knew many people who were unselfconscious enough to do that—especially with somebody who was purported to be a world-famous movie star.

"You'll be fine," she murmured.

He smiled again, surreptitiously inhaling the bouquet of her perfume. "I already am. Or I will be when I get you someplace safe, anyway. I have a feeling I should know what to do about stuff like this."

"It is too bad your memory isn't working," she mused, settling on the bed so that he could feel the heat of her against his side. "This reminds me of another movie we could make use of. *Home from the Sea.*"

"Mine?"

"Uh huh. You were kidnaped by terrorists who needed the computers you designed to rule the world...or something."

"Memorable flick, huh?"

He heard the grin without opening his eyes. "Actually, it was. You were a family man who only wanted to stay in your house in Indianapolis. You were kidnaped on board a yacht, along with the President of the United States. Pretty much saved the world with your brain instead of a gun."

"In a tux?"

She chuckled. "Afraid so."

He shook his head. "Cinéma-vérité, huh? How'd I get us out of it?"

"Reprogramed the ship's computers from the bathroom after being blinded by a bullet. You were pretty amazing."

For some reason, that made him frustrated. "It wasn't me."

She touched him again, a hand to his shoulder. "Oh, I know. Your character, I mean. But you chose the role. You played it. It says something about you."

"It says, evidently, that I like to spend my time in a tuxedo."

For that he got a moment of silence. "You don't sound as if it makes you think highly of yourself."

She was right. That was how he sounded. He wondered what it meant. He wondered what, when he finally cleared out the fog that muddled his thoughts and displaced his memories, he would think of the person he discovered lurking back there.

"Do you know that you have an Academy Award?" she asked gently.

He answered instinctively. "It isn't mine." Then he reached up to lift the rag from his eyes. That had meant something. It meant more than misplaced humility. "Neither is Cameron Ross."

Lilly was watching him, her face a soft, round blur against the diffuse afternoon light that poured in through the windows. He couldn't see well, but he could discern her concern. It made him, for the first time, frightened.

"That doesn't belong to me," he insisted. "I don't know why. But it doesn't. I'm someone else."

"A different name," she suggested. "I don't know that much about you, but could Cameron Ross be a...like, a stage name?"

A thread of tension broke in his chest. "Yes." It was right. "Yes, it is. But it's still not mine."

She shrugged, still sincerely distressed. "I don't know what else to call you."

"It's okay to call me Cameron," he said, knowing that, too, was somehow right. "But I don't think of myself that way. Neither does he."

"Who?"

He opened his mouth to say something. Some name. Some face. Nothing came out. He closed his eyes again and tried to ignore the panic that was crowding out the comfort of her presence. "I don't know. I just know that it's important. It has to do with why I'm on the boat. Why I've been snatched instead."

"Instead of what?"

Her hand. On his chest, resting as lightly as a breeze. Warming him, calming him, letting him know that no matter what he could or couldn't remember, no matter what was wrong or lost or in danger, she was there with him. Instinctively, he reached up to take hold of it and anchor himself there.

"I don't know," he admitted. "I don't seem to know much."

She held on tight. Leaned closer. "It's okay. It'll all come back, you'll see. For now, though, let's just pretend. We'll pretend you're Cameron Ross so you have a name. So you know how to react to people."

"And who will you pretend to be?" he asked.

There was tension in her fingers, even if her voice was just as soft and soothing. "I never learned to pretend for a living, Mr. Ross. I'm just me."

He opened his eyes. Considered the face that hovered over him like a soft, bronze moon. The eyes wide, dark and deep. The hair, black as night and tumbled around bare shoulders. The soft, full body tucked into a bright red swimsuit. An impressionist portrait of femininity. A dream of comfort and life. The smile of the sun and the water holding his hand.

"You're perfectly fine, Lilly," he assured her, lifting his free hand to her soft face. "Perfectly fine just the way you are."

Her teeth flashed against her tanned skin. "You did get hit on the head, Mr. Ross. Tell you what. You just close your eyes. I'm going to rummage around and see if I can find some first aid supplies, since they sank mine with my boat. If you don't do something about those cuts and bruises, you're going to have some scars you don't want."

Her voice sounded breathless, almost upset. He couldn't place it. But when she pulled away, she did it gently, so she didn't hurt him. What surprised him more was that it did hurt. Ached, as if he'd been separated from something vital.

"You the oldest in your family, too, Miss Kokoa?" he asked.

She halted. Waited. Smiled again, as if surprised. "As a matter of fact, I am. Terminal caregiver, that's me. And you don't need to call me that," she said. "Especially after what we've just been through. Please call me Lilly."

"I had much the same thought."

"You want to be called Lilly?"

For the first time since he'd found himself in the raft, he laughed. Really laughed. Even though it hurt like knives, it felt familiar, healing, as if he resorted to it in times of stress. Which, considering the circumstances, was probably appropriate.

"I may be called many things," he assured her. "I sincerely doubt Lilly is one of them. I guess Cameron will do. Or hey you. Or whosits."

"Whosits it is," she agreed. "Now, close your eyes and rest. I'll be right back."

"Lilly?"

She stopped. "Yes?"

He tried to make his smile nonchalant. He knew, without seeing her, that she wouldn't be fooled. "While you're scrounging up supplies, could you find some aspirin? And maybe some food? I have a feeling that part of my problem is bad nutrition.''

She huffed, as if impatient. ''I should have thought of that. Not a lot to eat on a life raft, huh?''

''Why should you have thought about it?'' he demanded. ''Are you trained for finding strange guys on life rafts?''

He at least got a little chuckle out of her. ''Sure. Standard Hawaiian schooling for all the dumb *haoles* who can't paddle a canoe. Now, close your eyes for a little while, while I figure this out.''

He did. Even so, he held on to the sound of her, the soft pad of her feet, the throaty hum of her voice as she moved. He didn't want to let her out of his reach. And not just because she was the only thing he was certain of—because she was something he thought he hadn't seen much of. She was someone he thought he shouldn't let loose, like a rare bird sighted in the high branches of a backyard tree.

Lilly. Flower of rebirth. Sweet and tough and bold at once. He liked the image. He liked the woman. He lay with his eyes closed and just drifted on the nearness of her.

He was scaring her. Not just by the fact that he still couldn't remember, still couldn't see, but by the fact that he was making her so comfortable around him. So committed and concerned.

She'd been stroking his face. Lilly didn't do that. Not to anybody but the people she loved. She knew better. The world wasn't comfortable with touchers. Her Tutu Mary had been a world-class toucher, with hands like miracles, soft and bright and healing. *Kahuna*'s hands. But Lilly didn't have *kahuna* hands. No one did anymore.

Lilly just had the instincts bred of a dozen generations of healers, whether she admitted it or not.

For a moment she just stood at the bottom of the bed and stared at him. Just considered what she'd gotten herself into. Lilly Kokoa, librarian extraordinaire, Mike and Wanda Kokoa's little girl, who knew everybody on the north shore and wanted nothing more in her life than to live near her family and practice a trade that didn't involve wearing a grass skirt in front of strangers. And suddenly she was stuck in the middle of a movie plot with kidnapers and international movie stars in tuxedos. The Lilly who had left Oahu four days earlier would have laughed at the idea. The Lilly who stood on the carpeted deck of a luxury cruiser, staring down at the compelling features of a man she barely knew, didn't.

Lilly wasn't a dreamer. Lilly knew what her life would be. She'd known it from the first moment her mother had said, "Lilly, child, somehow all those beautiful genes of your ancestors mixed up just a little wrong on you." The reactions of the boys she'd known had borne it out, and the world at large had cemented it. Lilly, whose sister had been a finalist for Miss Hawaii, was plain. She was a young woman with a better brain than a face, and a pragmatism that balanced with age-old instincts that still made people nervous. But Lilly didn't mind. She didn't need what she didn't have and cherished what she did. Which was her family and her interests and her home.

But Lilly wasn't a savior. She wasn't an action heroine. She wasn't a Bond girl.

So what the heck was she doing here trying to save a man who wouldn't have so much as noticed her if he'd come across her any place else? More important, what was she doing being so afraid for him, as if he meant something to her?

It's those feet, she said to herself with a wry smile she didn't feel. I go to do my good deed for the day and find myself obsessing over naked toes.

And hands. And wry, sweet, unfocused eyes the color of deep ocean.

Lilly shook her head as if she were shaking off water and headed for the bathroom to try to scare up some supplies. She should have been laughing at her ridiculous predicament. Instead she was praying.

"You've been shot!"

"I was thinking..."

Lilly looked up from the wound she'd just exposed. "Did you listen to me? I said you've been shot."

Positioned with his back against the headboard, his head already circled in a dramatic slash of white gauze, Cameron Ross flashed her an easy grin. "I heard you. Since I'm still alive and my leg seems intact, I imagine it's all right."

Lilly wanted to cry. She wanted to run. She was way out of her league here, and it just kept getting worse.

"No, it is not all right," she insisted. "You can hardly stand up, you have a concussion, and now I find out you've been shot. How can that be okay?"

He smiled like a little boy. "I'm alive," he said. "Considering the alternatives, that's not bad. Now, are you going to listen?"

Lilly took a second to shut him away beyond closed eyelids. She was tired already, and she'd just been up today. Not out in a life raft for two days. She'd let Cameron sleep for two hours, and he looked more alert than she felt. It wasn't fair. And that didn't even take into account the problem at hand, which was the extent of the injuries he'd sustained. Considering how battered and bruised he looked, he should be semi-comatose.

Lilly took another look at the angry gash in his thigh, where the bullet had entered. The salt water hadn't hurt it, but the time hadn't helped. Lilly couldn't think of anything else to do than what she'd already done for his head. Hydrogen peroxide, antibiotic ointment and a dressing. Trying to ignore the fact that her hands were shaking, she set to work.

And did her best to ignore the hard ridges of muscle in that thigh. The flat, washboard abdomen only inches north.

Everything else in between.

Lilly shut her eyes again. This was insane. She was losing her mind, terrified one minute, lusting the next. Or maybe the same. She couldn't tell anymore. She just knew she should never have told him to strip off that tux. Now he was lounging on the bed in boxers and bandages, and she was in more trouble than ever.

"Lilly?"

Silk boxers. With cartoon figures of Tweety Bird and Daffy Duck and Marvin the Martian, who all seemed to be laughing at her.

She refused to open her eyes. "Yes."

"You're not getting sick on me, are you?"

If only it were that simple. "No."

"How soon is the storm coming?"

That did get her to look at him. Lounging back on that bed, lean and male and magnificent, even with those unfocused eyes and all the bruising and abrasions starkly set against too-pale skin. "What?"

He smiled, as if it would help coax the information free. "When was the next storm expected?"

Distracted, Lilly took a look out the window, where the

sun was sinking in a red haze to the west. So instinctive was her adjustment to the feel of the increasing swell beneath her that she hadn't even noticed it. "I don't know," she admitted. "Tonight sometime. Maybe early morning."

"You mean you can't read the waves or anything? I thought you said you were Hawaiian."

She spun on him, ready to snap, only to see the glint of humor in his eyes. Here he was injured, held captive, and he was trying to make her feel better. She could fall in love with a guy like this.

Good thing she knew better.

She managed a none-too-enthusiastic grin. "We Kokoas have the distinction of being the only Hawaiians ever to sink our outrigger."

"A fine one to be making cracks about us *haoles*."

She wanted to giggle. The problem was, if she giggled, she would never stop. Her hands were shaking, and she wanted to vomit. And he was the one with the head injury.

"My Portuguese ancestors, on the other hand, landed on Hawaii during a storm just like this one…well, they didn't land so much as smash into the shore."

"Quite a family tree." His grin was still light and easy, and Lilly wanted to play along. Until his next declaration. "I figure we can use the storm to get free."

Lilly had been all set to clean his leg. That brought her attention sharply back. "We can *what?*"

That grin again, brash and fearless, as if he weren't darn near horizontal from the last try. "Well, it worked before. Why not again?"

"It did *not* work before," she retorted. "You're right back where you started. Only this time you're working on only one leg and half a brain."

"Ah, that's okay," he assured her. "I have a feeling

I've never worked on more than half a brain before anyway. What kind of distraction can we provide?''

That brought her to her feet, balled fists on hips. ''Don't do this,'' she insisted. ''We should wait here. Find out what's going on. Wait until the ransom is paid, and then we'll be released.''

She tried very hard to face down his skepticism. It didn't work.

''Is that how the movie came out?'' he asked gently. ''The one where I'm kidnaped? Did the kidnapers let the president go after the ransom was paid?''

Lilly stared out the window. ''It was just a movie.''

Biting back an oath at the effort it took, Cameron launched himself up to sit, his legs hanging off the side of the bed. ''I may not remember much, Lilly,'' he told her, his eyes empty of that mad sparkle, ''but I think I remember that if a kidnaper is going to let his victims go, he generally tries really hard not to let them see his face.''

Well, *that* made her feel better. ''I know.''

''Then you know we have to get out of here.''

That brought her head up. ''How?''

He looked around as if he could actually focus. ''I don't know. Let's check out the room and see if we find anything. Who knows? Maybe the ship's computer system goes through here and I can reprogram it.''

''This isn't a movie, Cameron.''

He smiled. ''But I do know computers,'' he said. ''Find me one, and maybe I can do some damage.''

''You sit down,'' she said. ''I'll look.''

He shook his head and got unsteadily to his feet. ''No. We'll both look.''

Lilly took a look as every inch of his more than six feet uncoiled before her and found herself struggling for breath. ''Well, would you at least put some clothes on

first?'' she demanded. ''It's really hard to be serious about
this when the only thing you're wearing is Daffy Duck.''

She saw the real confusion in Cameron's eyes when
she said that. He looked down, as if trying to remember
what he would find. ''I could probably use a good mouth-
wash and a shave, too, couldn't I?'' he admitted ruefully.

Lilly almost laughed. His head couldn't be so banged
up that he didn't realize how stop-traffic-on-a-six-lane-
highway-gorgeous he was. Pecs and a six-pack, her sister
would have said. The Impossible Dream, was how Lilly
saw it. And topped off with a face that only seemed more
roguish with that stubble of beard he was affecting. Gentle
and wise and rare.

And she wasn't even going to consider his feet.

So she turned around and began searching the cabin.

The room would have been huge even if they'd been
on land. It was also clean. No, not clean. Almost sterile.
Devoid of little musses and dropped objects that signified
real occupation. Empty of personal photos or comfortable
clutter.

''Don't you know anybody well enough to hang their
picture?'' she asked.

There was a pause. ''I don't know.''

Lilly flinched. ''I'm sorry. You're right. Well, we won't
get any hints about the real Cameron Ross in this room.
I don't think he lives here.''

She got another pause, this one longer. Lilly turned to
see Cameron standing in the bathroom, balancing himself
with his hands against the sink, his consideration on the
man in the mirror.

''Familiar?'' she couldn't help but ask.

He didn't answer right away. Just kept staring. ''I don't
ever think it occurs to anyone that he won't recognize the
face he sees in the mirror.''

Lilly didn't even realize she was moving until she stood next to him in the bathroom door. "You mean it?"

She should have sounded less afraid. She shouldn't have reached out to touch him. But when he turned, she was right there, her hand on his arm. And he smiled. A smile that only hinted at the turmoil that must have been going on behind those sky-blue eyes.

"Kind of silly to be this afraid of somebody I'm supposed to know pretty well."

Lilly was a toucher, just like her *tutu* had been, and hers before her. So her natural instinct was to touch. To offer comfort. Without a qualm, she just rose on her toes and wrapped her arms around him.

And he held her, too, curling around her as if she were his last hold on sanity. As if he were reassuring himself with her reality to bolster his own.

"It's going to be okay," she insisted in a whisper, her cheek against his chest. "I promise."

His instinctive laugh was a rumble against her ear. "Don't make promises you can't keep, young lady."

Lilly pulled her head back and smiled for him. "But I can keep them," she said. "My ancestors were *kahunas*. The keepers of the secrets, who knew magic and medicine the likes of which we'll never know again. They knew things the world has lost, and in my dreams they share them with me. I know what's going to happen, and I know what isn't. And I know you're going to be okay."

She said it more for the soothing sound of a voice, any voice, to pull him away from whatever precipice on which he found himself balanced. She didn't realize how much she wanted to believe it, just this once. Just for him.

She didn't realize how her wish would affect him.

She did when he kissed her. Wrapped in his arms, tight against his chest, her body full and flush against his, her hands against his broad back, her head tilted and her eyes, impossibly, closed.

Lilly Kokoa had been a practical girl. She was a practical woman. For just a moment, though, a hairbreadth of time locked on the edge of disaster, she lost her logic and flew.

And then pulled gently away.

Her breathing was ragged, her skin on fire where it met his, her mind in a puddle. She saw only needy blue eyes, craggy, haggard cheeks, the beginnings of a beard that had left her own cheeks scrubbed. She heard the syncopated rasp of their breathing and knew exactly what she had to say.

"Um, there's...something I have to tell you...."

He didn't budge. Didn't loosen his hold or his need or his fine, sweet gaze. "What?"

At least he sounded as confused as she felt.

So she closed her eyes. "You're married."

Which was, of course, the exact moment that their kidnapers slammed through the cabin door and knocked her straight back into his arms.

Three

"What are you two up to in here?" Huey demanded, automatic pistol pointed at Lilly's back.

Cameron—though he still couldn't quite think of himself as Cameron—just held on to her, as if that could somehow protect her from a trio of inept kidnapers carrying more firepower than the Dallas police department.

"Trying to get his injuries taken care of," Lilly grated against his chest.

At least she wasn't trying to pull out of his arms. He was sure he didn't want her to, for the sole reason that these guys were itchy and unprofessional and might shoot. Not because she felt so healing there. Not because he could smell those flowers in her hair, or because he thought she had the softest skin he'd ever touched.

Which, of course, he shouldn't be feeling, since he was already married to somebody else.

Married.

Nothing came. No image, no feeling, no name. He knew he still hadn't lost that nagging feeling that he needed to be somewhere else, but the idea of a wife didn't cement any reason for it. He just felt antsy, as if he had to get home.

He looked at Duey and Louise lining up behind Huey and decided that his matrimonial status could wait.

"What do you want?" he asked as calmly as he could.

Huey smiled. "Financial security in troubled times. Peace on earth. A house in Jamaica the size of LAX. Got a problem with that?"

Cameron shook his head. "Every boy's dream."

Huey laughed and pulled the gun in to rest across his chest, which he could do, since his partners still had theirs trained on ground zero.

Louise snickered. "That what famous movie stars wear under their evening clothes these days?" she demanded.

He looked down to realize that he was still damn near naked. Standing there with Lilly in his arms. Able to smell that plumeria that drifted off her like smoke and struck by the most powerful urge just to sink his face in that silky hair of hers.

Maybe he'd been in a lot of movies where he'd pretended this happened, but he would bet it had never happened to him in real life.

"My personal comment on fashion," he said as evenly as he could.

He wanted to ask what they wanted. He was afraid to. Afraid they would demand that Lilly leave. Demand worse, when he knew damn well he didn't have the skills to prevent it.

He had the urge, the overwhelming reflex, to just lash out. Considering the fact that he still couldn't put his weight on his left leg, he knew how well that would work out.

Then Huey surprised him again.

"Who's Ethan?" Huey asked.

He lifted his head, stunned. "What?"

"Ya deaf? Who's Ethan?"

His answer was instinctive. "Me."

Lilly almost cracked his chin with the back of her head when she looked up. "You?"

"What are you talking about?" Huey demanded, the pistol back in place.

He didn't know. God, he just wanted to lie down for about four hours and figure it out. Tickle the rest of that memory loose. Figure out this married thing so he could get back to Lilly.

All he could do was close his eyes and hold his breath. *Ethan.*

It was his; more than Cameron, more than the tuxes, more than this ship. But he didn't know why. He didn't know how.

"His middle name," Lilly spoke up, turning carefully to face their captors.

"That don't make sense," Duey snapped.

"Shut up," Huey told him. "Makes perfect sense. The computer keeps asking for Ethan, like it's a password or something. Of course Cameron Ross isn't gonna just put his real name out there for the world." Then he turned to Lilly. "You sure?"

Lilly flashed him a smile. "You kidding? I've had Cameron Ross on my bedroom wall since I was twelve. I know more about him than his mother."

Huey scowled with meaning. "You know he's married?"

Cameron…no, Ethan. Ethan wanted to laugh. Didn't it

just figure he would be kidnaped by criminals who picked and chose their commandments?

"Of course I do," Lilly assured the man. "What kind of person you think I am?"

Louise's laugh said it all.

Lilly glared at the three of them. "You knocked me into him, you jerks. He wanted to clean up, and I was trying to get him into the bathroom on a leg that isn't working very well because *you* shot him."

All three looked down at the gauze and tape that circled Ethan's leg.

"Oh," Huey said, surprised. "Sorry."

Lilly sniffed. "You should be. Now get out so he can finish. It's getting pretty rank in here, and I doubt you're going to let me get any fresh air any time soon."

Obviously stunned at hearing that particular tone of voice coming from a kidnaping victim, Huey turned on Ethan with a little wave of his gun in Lilly's direction. "You let her talk to *you* like that?"

Ethan shrugged. "Back in Hollywood there are people who'd pay her for the privilege."

All three shook their heads in appalled disbelief.

"Next time the boss sends us out," Duey said, "I ain't goin' unless it's somebody normal."

"What boss?" Lilly asked.

All three guns went up. So did Ethan's hands.

"On the other hand," he said as easily as he could, "she *does* ask too many questions. Now, what is it you want? I'm running out of optimal standing time here."

Huey nodded briskly, as if that made perfect sense. "It's time for you to send another little note over the modem."

"Another...I sent a note?"

Huey scowled. "'Course you sent a note. Where the hell were you?"

"He doesn't know," Lilly said, her arm still around his waist. He wished it weren't to hold him up, but it was beginning to feel that way. "He can't remember much of anything."

All three laughed.

Her eyes flashed. "You think it's funny? I hope you don't need his password to get into the computer. He doesn't remember it. He has retrograde amnesia from his head injury."

Huey scowled heartily. "What are you?" he demanded. "A doctor?"

"An encyclopedia," she retorted.

"Lilly," Ethan cautioned, pulling her a little closer. Then he shrugged for his captors. "She's right. I remember stupid little things that make no sense. Nothing about me. And, I'm sorry to say, nothing about you."

"What do you remember?" Louise demanded.

"Cal Ripken's record-breaking game, the presidents of the United States, somebody named Sally who makes slam-bang fried chicken, Star Trek conventions..."

"Star Trek conventions?" everybody in the room demanded in unison.

All he could do was shrug. "Hey, I'm as puzzled as you are."

For some reason that seemed to convince Huey, who spent a few long moments scratching his chin with his gun.

"You don't remember the password?"

Ethan shrugged. "Didn't you get it from me the last time?"

Duey snorted like an overworked engine. "No, he

didn't. The boss had it, but we can't figure out how to get hold of—''

''Shut up,'' Huey snapped.

''There must be some other way,'' Ethan offered.

All three looked up at him. ''What?''

He managed what he figured was a pretty convincing shrug. ''I don't know. Let me look at it. Maybe something'll come to me.''

''You sure you don't know nothin' 'bout computers?'' Duey demanded.

''Is that what I told you?''

They nodded.

He refrained from smiling. ''Then I guess it's a good bet I haven't learned anything about them since I've been down here.''

More chin scratching, then a nod. ''Okay. We'll leave her down here, so I don't get mad and you don't get any funny ideas.''

Ethan shook his head. ''Any of *you* know computers?'' he asked.

''Does Mario Brothers count?'' Louise asked with a sneer in her partners' direction.

''Well, Lilly does,'' Ethan said. ''I need her to help me. But I give you my word. We'll both behave.''

All three guns rose again. ''And the only message you send is the one I tell you,'' Huey retorted.

Ethan raised his free hand. ''My word.''

Huey waved his gun. ''Get some pants on.''

''Y'know, it's awfully noisy out there,'' Ethan said about fifteen minutes later as they stood on the high-tech bridge of the yacht.

Lilly thought he was a master of understatement. The wind was running right up the scales, shrilling along the

wires and aerials, shattering the tops of the waves into
spray and chilling her to the bone just in the time it took
to maneuver their way from the cabin. The storm that had
been predicted scattered lightning along the horizon and
threatened to toss the boat on its side. Lilly was having
trouble keeping her own balance, much less shoring up
Ethan's.

Ethan.

Odd, she'd only heard the name fifteen minutes ago,
and yet already she couldn't think of him any other way.
While she hadn't been comfortable thinking of this man
as Cameron Ross, she could easily think of him as Ethan.
Probably because it was less intimidating. Much less overwhelming. Cameron Ross was an icon. A stellar phenom-
enon from another universe who looked just different
enough on the screen from this man to make Lilly want
to squint to get him back into focus.

But Ethan was merely a man in trouble. A handsome
man. A handsome, charismatic man with eyes the color
of the ocean out beyond the reef. But only a man who
needed her help.

She could help a man named Ethan without worrying
about reality. So, that quickly, he became Ethan.

"If you guys don't understand computers," she ven-
tured to say, "how can you run the ship?"

It was Duey who answered. "Aw, the boss programed
it all. We just have to steer it back and forth."

"But the storm..."

She got a glare. "You think I don't know how to steer
for a little weather?"

Lilly just shrugged. Maybe Ethan was right. They
should take their chances in an open life raft rather than
with these three.

"Lilly," he murmured alongside her, his forehead

pursed with worry, his face inches from the screen. "Check me out here, okay?"

She bent close. Funny how that quickly her universe compressed itself to his voice and touch.

He was bent over the screen, tapping erratically on the keyboard. "I think I'm screwing this up," he said. "I just can't see it. Will you check and let me know what it answers?"

The yacht shuddered as it smacked into a swell, and Ethan staggered. Lilly caught him against the console. "You want me to do the typing?"

He shook his head. "Nah."

"What about the password?" Louise demanded.

Ethan shrugged. "That's what we're working on."

"Sometime today," Huey suggested with a little nudge of his gun to the kidneys. "They're waiting."

These people were really straining Lilly's patience. "He can't see very well, either," she informed them. "From his head injury. Which you also gave him."

Louise didn't seem that concerned. "Life sucks, huh, honey?"

"No," Ethan muttered to himself. "That's not right either, is it? I was hoping the password was going to be *Home from the Sea.*"

Lilly looked closer. Ethan wasn't trying to access the modem. He was typing complex commands.

Home from the Sea. The movie in which the hero had sabotaged the computer system to save himself and the President of the United States from kidnapers. Lilly desperately hoped she was keeping a straight face. Her stomach had just hit the floor.

Please, she prayed, don't let them see the OK on the screen.

"Try it again," she said. "It doesn't look like the right macro."

Ethan nodded in frustration, but Lilly could see the muscle twitch at the corner of his mouth. He was enjoying this, damn it! No wonder he'd gotten shot.

"I just can't see this," he muttered, rubbing at his eyes in frustration.

A series of commands scrolled past, which meant he'd just initiated some process in the system. Lilly stepped closer so nobody else could see. "Come on, Ethan. Let me type this for you. We'll make better time."

He sighed like a martyr and took just long enough trading places with her to let the scrolling clear.

"Let me try a few names," she said as she finally saw the password prompt.

She got it on her third try.

"Pete?" Ethan echoed incredulously when she told him.

She grinned. "Your first starring role. In *Dream Time*. It's about a rodeo champion."

He sighed again, this time for real. "In a tux?"

She couldn't believe it. She giggled. "Chaps and spurs. It raised quite a few women's blood pressure."

"Raised mine," Louise admitted.

"The message," Huey all but growled. "Send it."

Lilly accessed the outmail box, retrieved the address of the last message and then read it. "Uh oh, I think we're in trouble."

Four heads moved closer. "What?"

Lilly looked at Ethan. "You sent them a piece of little-known information about yourself last time to prove your identity," she said. "What do we do?"

"Tell 'em you hit your head," Huey suggested. "You can't remember."

"They'd think you'd already killed me," Ethan said evenly. "You wouldn't get your money...it is money you're after, isn't it?"

"Is there anything else?"

Ethan turned back to Lilly with a frown. "What was the information?"

Lilly read it again and fought a silly urge to giggle. "You took ballet lessons?"

He was obviously as startled as she. "Couldn't prove it by how I've been moving since I met you."

"Try those Star Trek conventions," Huey suggested dryly.

Shaking his head, Ethan closed his eyes. Lilly immediately wanted to reach out, lay a hand against his cheek. Soothe him. Seduce the memories more easily from him. Somehow she knew that the threat to his memory terrified him much more than the threat to his life. She wanted to tell him it would be okay. Given time, he would find it again. Given the chance to get back to his family, he would remember them.

"What about your wife?" she asked quietly. "Dulcy."

His eyes opened. "Is that her name?"

Lilly couldn't manage much more than a nod. He looked so lost. So uncertain, when only moments before he'd been attacking this whole thing like a video game.

"Even I know her name," Huey snorted. "It won't work."

"Wait." That quickly, Ethan's eyes lit. "I do remember something. Pea Ridge, Virginia."

Lilly blinked. "Pardon?"

"Pea Ridge, Virginia."

"What's that?"

"I don't know. But it means something."

"Maybe it's where your wife was born."

"Or me."

"No. You were born in England."

This time, *he* blinked. "I was?"

"Get *on* with it!" Huey shouted.

Lilly got on with it. She typed the proof and then the message—a basic "leave the money in the third Dumpster in the second alley north of the International Market in Honolulu" kind of thing. She was about to hit the Send command when Ethan stopped her.

"Let me," he said. "I'd just feel less…impotent."

Lilly didn't know from impotent. She did know that for all his stuttering and posturing, he played a keyboard like a virtuoso. Maybe he couldn't see, but he knew what he was doing. It was just that she didn't.

"The message has been sent," she finally announced.

Huey leaned in to verify it. Then they waited for the response, which turned out to be a simple "Acknowledged."

Kind of anticlimactic, Lilly thought. She wondered whether Ethan's wife was at the other end of that transmission. She wondered why this Dulcy hadn't added a plea for his safety, a personal message meant just for him. A reassurance of love and support. She wondered, fleetingly, whether Ethan really had anyone worth him waiting at home, no matter what the press reported.

"Can I go back down below?" he asked, sounding suddenly tired. "I'm feeling pretty bad again."

Considering what had happened the last time, everybody scrambled. And then they locked the two of them in the suite.

"Okay," Lilly said as soon as she'd deposited him on the bed. "Spill it."

He was lying there with his arm under his head, grinning like the Cheshire Cat. "Spill what?"

"What exactly were we doing up there? There were a couple of times it looked like you were repositioning satellites."

He waved his free hand like a prestidigitator. "Pack your bags, Lilly. We're blowing this pop stand."

That wasn't what Lilly wanted to hear. "What did you do, Ethan?"

His smile faded a little. "Not Cameron?"

She shrugged. "I don't know. Is it dumb to say that it's easier to think of you as Ethan than as Cameron Ross?"

"Not if Cameron Ross is always running around in a tuxedo. As you can see," he said, motioning to the gray chinos and eggplant linen shirt he'd pulled on, "Ethan is not quite so sartorial."

"You don't mind?" she asked.

"I already told you," he assured her. "I *am* Ethan. I don't know exactly what that means, but it's my name. Now, I was serious about packing. Get yourself some clothes, Lilly. And whatever you think we might need to survive on that raft. In about fifteen minutes the power's going to shut down on this thing."

Lilly's courage suffered a serious setback. "With those three in charge, the boat will turtle."

"By which time you and I will be on the life raft paddling for shore, and our rescue forces will have been clued in on our exact position from our Navstar system....I wonder if I'm insured for loss of a yacht."

Lilly couldn't help but chuckle. "You could pay for this thing out of pocket change."

"Well, good. That's one problem taken care of." He was rubbing at his eyes again, his voice still sounding weary.

"Tell me what you want," Lilly said, standing up. "You rest."

"Nope," he said, not moving. "My plan. I have to help."

Lilly headed over to the closet, where she'd seen an athletic bag. Perfect size for lifesaving equipment. "There is a plan, then?"

"Sure. Wait 'til the ship's in danger, then climb out the windows. Head for the life raft."

Lilly turned, appalled. "That's it?"

"Simplicity is an advantage in escape plans and alibis."

She couldn't help but laugh. "That sounds like a line from a movie."

He laughed back. "It does, doesn't it? I must be an actor."

Lilly stood there for a minute, just watching him. There should have been something she could say. Some encouragement she could share with this man who had so managed to upend her life. And yet, though there was so much she wanted to say, she could say nothing.

"Lilly?"

She started like a rabbit. Somehow, while she'd been staring at him, he'd decided to open his eyes and look back at her.

"What?" She even sounded tentative. Afraid.

"I'm sorry."

Lilly wanted to move. To run from him. To run to him. She stood there like a lump. "Sorry? For what?"

His smile said it all.

She wanted to say something funny. Something that stole the terror and replaced it with bravado. Even something that negated the various unpleasant facts they were eventually going to have to face. Maybe that was just a little too much for her, though.

"I'm still trying to deal with the fact that this is all real," she offered instead, with a grin that should have been much broader.

Ethan sat up and motioned her over. Even knowing she shouldn't, she sat next to him.

"Whatever happens," he said, taking hold of her hand, "you saved my life. I'll never be able to thank you enough for that."

She knew she was trembling. "Well, heck, I didn't have anything else more interesting planned."

He lifted a hand to her hair, touching it so softly that Lilly could have imagined it. She ached to the tips of her toes with the contact.

"Ready to go?" he asked gently.

No. Never. For the first time in her life, Lilly wanted to give in to fantasy. She wanted to stay right here and pretend that this room was all there was in the world. Nothing else. No job. No demands. No wife.

No wife.

She really was in trouble, and she'd only known him a day.

"Yeah," she said, hoping he didn't see the tears. "Let's rock and roll."

She got to her feet and then, on terrible impulse, bent over and kissed him. Once. Because she knew damn well that it didn't matter whether they stayed on the yacht or made it to the life raft. They probably weren't going to get as far as sunrise. And then she turned away to finish packing.

They only had fifteen minutes. Less, if the storm hit early, since Lilly had the feeling that their captors didn't know as much about the sea as they thought. She shoved in warm things, sweatshirts, jeans, socks. A couple of light linen shirts like the one Ethan was wearing. Shorts. Shoes. It would have been nice if she could have found something to fit her size-six feet, but she figured if worse came to worse she could stick socks in the toes of Ethan's size-tens.

It briefly occurred to her that Ethan's wife must not be quite the sailor he was, since she didn't find any women's clothing here. Oh well, she would have to cinch up belts and roll up legs. And she needed to save room for some soap, some bottled water, hydrogen peroxide, more bandages. The rest she could find on the island, when they made it that far.

When. What a lovely word.

"Is there some secret about you nobody knows involving clumsiness?" she asked as she surveyed the array of first aid equipment in his medicine cabinet. "You're covered for everything but major surgery here."

Ethan turned; he was noshing a granola bar as he eased shoes on over his sunburned feet. "Maybe I was a Boy Scout."

"Nope."

She could hear the grin in his voice. "You really do know so much about me?"

Lilly had to laugh. "Even if I'd been in a coma these last four years I would have gotten that information through osmosis. You're the most popular thing in the world since Shirley Temple, pal."

He just shook his head. "Maybe there's a reason I can't remember any of this. Maybe I just don't want to."

Lilly looked up in surprise to see him rubbing at his head as he chewed. He didn't realize the import of what e'd just said. It had been a throwaway line, but Lilly vondered.

This wasn't the time to deal with it, though. The clock vas ticking down, the seas were getting more erratic, and niserable or not, that man was married. Lilly turned back o the medicine cabinet.

"Why would you need normal saline?" she asked. 'Volume replacement for when you fall through the win- .ow?"

"Contacts."

Lilly grabbed the antibiotic ointment instead. She didn't .otice the stunned silence behind her until it was too late.

"Oh, my God, Lilly, that's it!"

Lilly turned to see him jump to his feet and almost land n his nose as the boat heeled over.

"Ethan…"

He was yanking out the drawers in the bedside table as f trying to unearth intruders. "Here I've been thinking I an't see because of that conk on the head," he was say- ng as he tossed flashlights, books and condoms onto his ed in his haste to scrabble through the drawer. "But the est of me feels a lot better, and I still can't see a thing. think I just wear glasses!"

Lilly reacted instinctively. "No, you don't."

"I do!" he crowed, adding two ties, a jar of pennies nd a notepad that said Hilton Hotels on it to the pile on he bed. "I think I'm blind as a bat!"

"But how can you fly?"

He blinked. "I fly?"

"Your own jet."

He was already shaking his head. "I'm telling you, omewhere on this boat is a pair of pop-bottle-bottom lasses. Or contacts. Look for them, Lilly. I'm going to eed to see to get out of this all right." He turned on her, his grin wide and delighted. "Heck, I want to see you, Lilly."

Lilly's stomach did another dive. "Well, you've ju ruined *my* day," she said under her breath and wondere whether she would lose her lifesaving merit badge be cause she didn't want to look for the damn things at al She also didn't want to consider what a drawerful of co doms meant to a man traveling without his wife. So sh went back to gathering first aid equipment.

"Here they are!" he yelled behind her.

Lilly froze, her back to him. Stupid reaction. She kne what he would see. It was just that, for the first time i her life, she wished she could have switched places wit her sister Tai.

She couldn't help it. She sneaked a look over her shou der to see him slip on a pair of—he'd said it—pop-bottle bottom glasses.

"Oh, thank God," he breathed, looking at the Winslo Homer print on the wall in front of him. "I'm not goin to die of a brain injury. I'm just nearsighted.... Lilly..."

He was turning. There was no place she could run an hide. Lilly could only stand there in the bathroom doc with a bottle of peroxide in one hand and a box of Ban Aids in the other and wait for the inevitable.

Talk about divine intervention. Ethan had made it ha way around when the lights went out.

Lilly laughed. Then a wave broadsided the yacht an sent them both straight to the floor.

Four

Noah Campbell rubbed at the grit in his eyes and focused on the horizon. Water, more water, and more water than that, with angry dark clouds piling up along the horizon.

"Honey," Dulcy urged yet again. "Let Jack do the flying. You haven't had any rest since the first message came in."

Without taking his attention from the weather outside, he reached over his shoulder and patted her hand. "We're almost there, Dulcy."

"You're not going to do Ethan any good if you can't focus."

"We have the FBI to focus. All Ethan needs from me is my approval to get the money."

Dulcy rubbed at his tight shoulders. "He's alive, Noah. We're going to get him back."

Noah didn't even want to think about any other alternative. It was his fault Ethan was in danger. His fault that

Ethan could be dead. Three million dollars. God, he would have paid a hundred times that to get his cousin back.

Ethan had never failed him. Ethan, who had welcomed him as a brother when his mother had run. Ethan, who had shared his dreams and helped make them a reality. Ethan, who had spent most of his adult life protecting Noah's identity and preserving his sanity.

Noah owed him more than money. He owed Ethan his life. He would gladly give it if he could just spare Ethan this nightmare.

"I know," Dulcy whispered behind him as if she'd heard every thought. "I know."

Noah fought the panic that closed his throat and held on to her hand. "We'll be there soon."

Jack leaned in the door behind Dulcy. "Boss, the second message just came in. Pea Ridge, Virginia, mean anything to you?"

Noah couldn't help but smile. Pea Ridge had been where he and Ethan had first hatched the plans that would set them both up for life. Sitting out on the porch roof after dark, making promises only young boys thought possible.

"Together, Noah. Like the musketeers."

"The musketeers."

"You make the movies. I'll make the money."

"And we'll both spend it."

"On cars."

"And planes."

"A big house in the city for my mom."

"And a house in the mountains for us."

It had been Ethan who'd shaken his head. *"No more mountains for me, cuz. Never again. I'll get your mountains for you, though."*

And he had. Noah had put Ethan through business

school on his earnings from stunt work, and Ethan had put Noah into the realms of the super-rich with his savvy handling of Noah's paychecks.

Ethan had bought Noah his mountains.

And, in return, Noah had gotten Ethan kidnaped. Maybe killed.

"Yeah," he said. "Pea Ridge is legitimate."

"Okay then, I'll tell the FBI to accept the message as valid. Also, I just got word from back home. Two things. Ellen's about three hours behind you and furious you didn't wait for her."

Noah shook his head. "I probably shouldn't have called her at all. She's just going to be upset."

"And she wasn't going to be upset if you didn't tell her at all?" Dulcy asked with a soft laugh. "You know better than that, Noah."

He sighed. Yeah, he knew better. But he didn't deal all that well with Ellen.

"The other thing?" he asked, putting that problem off as long as he could.

Jack sighed himself. "Somebody saw you board at Santa Monica. The word's out."

Noah looked over his shoulder at the square-jawed pilot towering over his tiny wife. "You sure Ellen didn't break the news just to get back at me?"

"Ellen would never jeopardize Ethan," Dulcy said. "You know that. Now, ease up on her a little, or you're never going to be able to be in the same room with her again."

Noah returned his focus to his flying, even though the autopilot was on and his course set. "What do the authorities think we should do?"

"They'll talk to you when you land," Jack said. "I think they want you to announce the truth."

Noah never hesitated. "Of course. Anything." Only then did he think to look to Dulcy. "I'm sorry, Dulce...."

She was already shaking her head. "Don't be sorry. Get Ethan back."

God, he loved her. Ethan had shown him that, too.

For a minute, he shared that with his wife. His beautiful, headstrong, sweet wife who would give up her privacy without a thought for the sake of her cousin-in-law.

"Message sent and acknowledged," Jack said, poking his head back in the cabin. "Something else. It looks like your cousin is okay. He was playing with the computers. Tried to link the message to their position on their navigation system."

Both Noah and Dulcy looked up. "Tried?"

Jack shrugged. "The message cut off before we could get a true fix."

Five

"**I**'m not sure this is such a good idea," Lilly objected.

Ethan did his best to keep his balance as the ship plunged and rolled in another growing swell. "It did sound a heck of a lot better when I still had glasses."

"I'm really sorry about that," she apologized as the two of them manhandled the two-man life raft to the edge of the deck. "I was trying to make sure you were okay."

The rain had started—heavy, driving pellets that stung Ethan's eyes and effectively blinded him. Well, blinded him more. It was dark, he had no focus and there was water in his eyes. And somewhere on this ship, there were three kidnapers who weren't going to take much more time to realize that he and Lilly had gotten out.

"Come on!" he yelled over the driving rain. "One more push. I'll hold on to the rope. You jump and get in first."

"Do you want me to take the paddles?"

"I want you to take the outboard. Too bad Huey stole it."

He thought she grinned. "Too bad he didn't count on Island Girl, here. Paddling's easier in these swells."

Ethan thought briefly that she shouldn't ever try to get a job acting. Her voice was thick with terror. "You weren't the Kokoa who sank the outrigger, were you?"

"Nah. That was Great-Great-Uncle Mano. I'm a whiz. Can you swim?"

"We'll find out."

They did. But not before they were discovered.

It was Louise who caught them, just as they were going over the side.

"Where the hell you think you're going?" she shrilled, lifting her gun.

Ethan didn't take time to think. He just shoved Lilly off into the water and the life raft right after her.

"Hold it!" Louise demanded, running for him.

He could hardly stand up. The deck was slippery, the wind was shoving him horizontal, and he was trying his damnedest to focus on the sounds of Lilly below him. God, he hoped she'd made it into that boat.

Then he heard the stutter of Louise's gun, and he knew he couldn't wait any longer. One hand on the supply-stuffed gym bag and the other on the lifeboat rope, he ran toward the side. He'd just about gotten there when he heard a funny cry behind him. He turned, only to have Louise skid into him full tilt. She knocked him against the brass railing just as the gun went off again. Pain exploded in his head and his side.

Not again, was all he could think as he went freewheeling over the side of the boat.

Lilly saw him fall. She had just clambered on to the raft, which was pitching like a ride at Disneyland, and was trying to right herself. She heard Louise, then the distant stutter of a weapon, and then she saw two bodies hurtling into the water from the side of the yacht.

"Ethan!" she screamed, lunging for her end of the boat rope.

There was still tension on it. Wherever he was, at least he hadn't let go. Lilly hauled as hard as she could. The waves tossed the little boat around like a bathtub toy, then dropped it hard. Lilly repositioned herself for better balance and held on tighter.

"Don't let go," she begged as if he could hear her. "Just don't let go."

He didn't. She saw his hand first, gleaming in the lightning as it clamped on to the side of the inflatable raft. Letting go of the rope with a sob, she tried her best to balance the boat and help him haul himself in.

"Are you okay?" she demanded, getting a grip on a belt loop and yanking with all her might.

Coughing and retching, he flopped in next to her like a landed carp. "Lilly," he gasped, openmouthed. "I want to...thank you for break...breaking my glasses...."

Lilly didn't know whether to laugh or scream. "I *told* you I didn't mean it!"

Damn it if he didn't grin, lying there trying so hard to get his breath. "No, I mean it. I don't think I wanted to see what I just did."

She laughed. Hard. Then she bent over and just held on to him. And almost got them capsized all over again.

Reassured by the wet, laughing comfort of him, Lilly straightened. "Are you okay?" she asked.

"Yeah."

"You're bleeding again."

He waved a hand. "No problem."

"You sure?"

"Yeah. You're right. I must be a klutz. Hit my head again."

That almost propelled Lilly right to her feet. "What do you mean, you hit your head again?"

"Lilly," he cautioned, his voice soft despite the cacophony around them. "It'll wait. Right now, I think we need to be doing something more productive. Don't you?"

Lilly looked around. They were already moving away from the yacht, which she could make out as a gray rectangle against the furious white of the waves. She couldn't see much else, but she'd gotten a fix on the mountains of Molokai before Ethan had pushed her off the side of the boat.

"I'll paddle," she decided with a less-than-assured grin. "You bail."

He lifted his sodden Stetson from the floor of the raft. "What do you think I brought this along for?"

She couldn't help snorting. "Old time's sake. After all, you don't have your tux."

Lilly was snapping the oars into the gunwale when she saw another hand clamp onto the side of the boat. A shudder of lightning betrayed a head lifting from the water right behind it. A head with thick black hair and furious eyes.

Louise.

Lilly was so surprised at seeing the woman, she couldn't seem to even cry out. She just found herself lifting the paddle in defense. Then she saw the gun Louise was lifting and realized it was pointed dead center at Ethan.

"No!" she screamed and slashed down as hard as she could with the flat end of the oar. "Ethan, duck!"

Lilly heard the sick, flat thunk of that oar hitting a skull. She saw those furious eyes widen in surprise. She saw hand and head and gun disappear.

"Oh, my God!" she cried, dropping the oar. "I think I killed her!"

She probably would have leapt over the side of the boat if Ethan hadn't caught her. "Lilly, stop! You just saved my life again. Don't ruin the effect!"

Lilly whipped around to see him still crumpled in the bottom of the boat, blood on his face, his breathing erratic and shallow. And still—still—he was trying to laugh.

"This isn't funny!" she protested, tears in her eyes. "She's going to drown!"

"And if you save her, she's going to shoot us." Thunder clapped against the water, rain drove sideways against Lilly's face, and she saw that Ethan, even in a jacket, was shivering. "We've got to get to shore, Lilly, or all our work will be wasted."

Still she couldn't move, even with the lightning tearing apart the sky and the waves so high that the cruiser completely disappeared on the other side. Even with the wind shredding her skin with salt-spiked spray, she couldn't seem to do more than clutch that damn oar and stare at Ethan.

Who smiled.

As if he were in somebody's living room discussing ethics. As if he'd just witnessed a small faux pas and forgiven it. Lilly shook, and Ethan reached over to touch her hand. "Lilly, we have to go," was all he said, and yet, in those words, she found comfort. She gained movement and forward momentum.

She sobbed once, because she'd never in her life caused deliberate harm to another human, and then she finished setting the last oar.

Beside her, Ethan chuckled. "You sure I'm the action hero on this boat?"

Lilly wanted to laugh. Even with tears running down her cheeks and chills chasing through her like a train through a tunnel. "Bail, buddy," she instructed instead. "I'll row."

She rowed. She rowed hard, fighting the wind, the waves and the current. She heard long before Ethan did the terrible roar of the surf against the rocks that littered the north coast of Molokai. She knew far better than he that if she didn't manage to steer this little amusement-park ride correctly, they would end up as so much shark-bait.

Even with the oversized windbreaker she'd taken from Ethan's closet, Lilly was soaked and freezing. She was terrified Ethan wasn't moving as well as he should. She was straining every muscle in her back and arms to keep that little boat moving in the right direction. And then, when she thought she couldn't take another surprise, Ethan began to sing.

Opera.

Beautifully.

Lilly almost forgot to row. "You sing?" she demanded.

Lounging against the side and rhythmically lifting the Stetson over the edge to dump it out as if he weren't inches from disaster, he shrugged. "I guess so. Do you know it?"

"*La donna è mobile,*" she said. "Nice choice. It sets up the perfect rowing and bailing rhythm. But you never told anybody you could sing."

His teeth flashed white in the dark. "Well, now you know something the world doesn't."

So while she rowed, he sang. Not loudly. Not with the control or gusto Lilly had a feeling he usually imbued into his music. But with a clear, sweet tenor voice that was lovely enough that Lilly almost forgot their predicament as she matched her strokes to the easy, loping rhythm of the piece.

And then, unbelievably enough, she found herself singing along.

Which brought Ethan to a sudden, surprised stop. "You know opera?"

She scowled. "As amazing as that may seem, we sing more in Hawaii than *Aloha Hoi* and *Tiny Bubbles*."

He laughed, still bailing. "I guess I've spent so many years explaining my tastes that I'm surprised anybody else shares them."

It was all Lilly could do to keep rowing. "Keep that thought," she said.

She thought his eyes widened in surprise. "I remembered something, didn't I?"

"You remembered the words to *La donna è mobile*," she assured him with a laugh. "I'd say that's pretty impressive."

For minutes, hours, eternities, they fought the waves, the storm and the wind. Lilly thought she was going to die from the exertion. She even dallied with the thought that she wished she'd been the one with the head injury so she could bail instead of row. But she heard the roaring grow closer. She knew they were nearing land, which was either going to be very good news or the last news they ever heard. And then Ethan cinched it in one.

"I think we have another problem, Lilly."

"I don't...want another...problem, Ethan."

"The boat's deflating."

That did it. They were going to have a tough enough time getting through the surf in an intact boat. They didn't stand a chance now.

"I think Louise must have kept her finger on the trigger as she went over the side of the boat. More then one of the compartments is deflating. I think you're lucky she didn't hit you."

Lilly figured it wouldn't make a difference in about twenty minutes.

"Hear that surf?" she asked.

"I can actually see that surf," he assured her. "We gonna make it through?"

She sighed. "Probably not. You want to try and tie the supplies to us just in case, though?"

Somehow Ethan managed to keep bailing as he cut the boat's rope and tied the athletic bag around his waist. He'd no sooner finished than Lilly felt the surf catch them. And he was right. The boat was deflating. It didn't skim over the water as it should have. It wallowed. Water poured in and soaked her. She could hear Ethan choking.

"Hang on!" she yelled and strained to propel the boat forward.

They almost made it. Lilly rowed and Ethan bailed and the boat bucked and lurched like a drunken animal. Lilly tried her best to watch over her shoulder and steer them past the guardian rocks. The water writhed and thundered like a malevolent being. The wind howled, and Lilly prayed. The boat swept up so fast that Lilly's stomach took a second to follow. And then, just when she thought she saw beach, the wave tumbled and spilled them out into the surf.

She didn't know how he did it, but Ethan caught hold of her. They were tumbled and spun and slammed into the sand, and he didn't let loose. Lilly fought the undertow with arms and legs long used to strong currents. She somehow instinctively kept her sense of direction and kicked for land. Her lungs were on fire. Her whole body hurt from the pummeling she was taking. She thought, finally, that she wasn't going to make it, just as the surf spat her out like a bad-tasting leftover.

"Ethan!"

Unbelievably, he was still moving. "Right here."

Lilly wasn't sure who dragged whom, but they got each other far enough away from the surf to survive. And then, completely exhausted, they collapsed onto the sand.

"So," he managed, coughing again, his free hand to his chest. "This is Hawaii."

Lilly started laughing and couldn't stop. Over her head, the trees writhed against a lightning-charged sky. The ocean thundered and the wind screamed. And somehow, with a boat that was now nothing more than a deflating balloon, they had made it.

"We're going to need to get to shelter," she said, closing her eyes against the rain that was beginning to slacken.

"Uh huh."

"We could catch pneumonia here."

"Uh huh."

He had hold of her hand as if afraid one of them would be swept off the land by a freak burst of wind.

"We could be hit on the head with flying coconuts."

This time he didn't answer at all. Lilly knew she should turn and make sure he was okay. She couldn't muster the energy. She was cold and wet and aching in a hundred places. And yet, lying on a small strip of beach at the edge of the ocean in a full gale, she fell asleep.

Six

He might not remember much, but Ethan bet he'd never been in a position like this before. He knew it even before he opened his eyes. He could hear birds crying and insects chittering. Sunlight warmed his eyelids. A soft wind rustled in overhead trees, and somewhere close water pounded against a shoreline. And his shorts were full of sand.

He should move. He should at least investigate all the various sharp and dull pains that had set up in his body. He couldn't dredge up the energy. The rain had stopped, he was on dry land, and somehow he'd ended up with a woman in his arms.

Even that felt strange. Alien, as if he weren't used to it, which he should have been, if he was married like they'd all told him. That didn't change the sweet comfort of it, though, the sense of long-sought solace. Even over the salt of the ocean, the dark loam of the forest, the stench of fish, he could smell the flowers in Lilly's hair. He could feel the oh, so soft pressure of her breasts against his oh, so sore chest. He could hear the soft wash of her breath as it fanned his throat. And he simply didn't want to move.

Maybe he didn't want his memory back. Not if it meant giving this up. Not if it meant he had to move for propriety's sake, or regret giving Lilly away because he couldn't bear to hurt someone he loved.

Again, he sought a memory. Any memory.

Dulcy. They'd said her name was Dulcy. He did know somebody named Dulcy. Someone small and redheaded and fiery. He could see her in the mountains, and that didn't make sense. He didn't like the mountains. He was an ocean man.

Then why did he remember a ranch? The Flying W. And Dulcy.

And nothing else.

No sense of loving her. Of her fitting against his side like Lilly did. No sense that she meshed with the frail image that was beginning to focus within him of who he was.

Again he felt the pull to be somewhere else. To be moving, as if he were late. But not as if he were missed.

Everybody else seemed so sure of who he was. Why couldn't he be?

"Ethan?"

Lilly's voice was sleepy, uncertain.

Ethan was very careful not to react. He knew he was a coward, maybe a faithless bastard. But he simply didn't want to give away the only comfort he'd known since waking up in this strange body.

"You alive, too, Lil?"

She was just as careful as he not to move. He wondered, selfishly, if she didn't want to let go, either.

"We should get up to shelter," she said in a small voice.

"Nah. Let's just stay here. I gave the good guys an idea of where we might be. We just have to wait to flag 'em down."

Besides, if they moved, he would lose his excuse to wrap himself around her softness. To fill himself with the smell and taste and feel of her. God, he wished he could see her, see those faint, fleeting expressions he was sure he would catch in her eyes. The flawless bronze of her skin. The arch of eyebrow and cheekbone, the delicate throb of a pulse at her throat.

He could feel her hips against his, full, luxuriant hips that promised lush love and lusty children. He could feel the impossibly sweet pressure of those breasts against him. Proud, full, high breasts, with nipples the color of pennies, he bet. Made to fill a man's eyes with delight and his mouth with madness. He could smell the flowers on her thick silky hair, the darker, earthier musk of woman on her skin. He could almost taste the salt on her throat and the honey of her eyes.

But he couldn't see her. Not far away. Not close. It didn't seem to matter to his eyes, which distorted everything. Even with glasses on. He hadn't told her, of course. He hadn't wanted her to worry. But there had still been a kind of film over his eyes, even with the edges clearing. And so he had to think that this was all he would ever get. Lilly in the mist. And he ached to see not just wide dark pools where eyes should be, but the eyes themselves, the colors, the emotions, the sunlight of laughter. He itched to run his hands over what he saw to cement it in his mind.

Probably a good thing he couldn't see after all. Then for sure he would never again want to take his hands off her.

He kept very still, so she couldn't object; he was only touching her where they met, hip to hip and cheek to chest on the sand.

"And if our friends kept the boat afloat last night?" she asked. "They'll know where we are, too. Besides, it's going to rain again. It always rains on this side of the island. And it's *Mahoa Mua.*"

He wanted so badly to run his fingers through her hair. He didn't. "*Mahoa Mua?* What's that?"

"Hawaiian calendar. The month of sudden storms." He could feel her face form into a grin against his chest. "To you *haoles,* middle of August to the middle of September. We're still barely in August."

August. Late summer. He tried to put some task or treat to the month and couldn't come up with anything, except that summer vacation was almost over.

Which was probably as appropriate an analogy as any, he thought with unaccountable regret.

"Tell you what," he offered. "If we spot the cruiser, we'll head on inland. If not, we just stay here under a tree."

"There's a two-way radio in the cabin," she urged.

"Cabin?" he asked. "What cabin?"

"It's where I was on my way home from when we ran into each other. My family lived in these valleys for generations. Now we just have an old hunting cabin my uncles keep up."

Ethan considered the perilously narrow blur of light that

represented the total span of the sky above them. "This isn't a valley," he assured her. "It's a chasm. There's no way I'm going to be able to get up it."

She snorted. "People have been climbing this valley for centuries. Father Damien used to be set down here to get over the hills to his people on the peninsula."

"Father Damien?"

"Sure. You never heard of the leper colony on Molokai? It's about three volcanic ridges over."

"It's still there?"

He thought she grinned. "You'd think you westerners would read up on the place before you visited, y'know?"

Ethan wanted to smile back. "Hey, maybe I did. I could have stored that information away with the last four films I made."

For a moment there was silence. Ethan watched the impressionistic dance of tree patterns dipping and swaying over his head. He listened to the life that crowded the vegetation that spilled over what was undoubtedly vertical cliffside and smelled the gingery bouquet of its aroma. It was lovely and exotic and wild here.

And empty. No people. No phones. No pressure.

"Y'know," he mused out loud. "Except for the fact that I don't think I'll ever walk again, this would win my vote as the perfect fantasy getaway."

Lilly stirred a bit. "You like it here?"

He liked *her* here. He liked her voice and her touch and her anxious concern. And he liked the place that had created her.

"Oddly enough, I do," he said. "Especially considering the fact that I don't like mountains."

"You don't like mountains? Why?"

He shrugged and regretted the movement in at least

three ribs and a shoulder. "Don't know. I just know that I vowed never to go back to the mountains again. I'm an ocean man."

For a moment she was quiet. He thought she was smiling again, but her voice didn't sound quite as happy. "Well, fortunately for you, then, we are happy also to provide a very lovely ocean."

"It is lovely," he admitted. "Now that I'm not lost in the middle of it with no way off."

"*Kanaloa* can be a pretty tough god sometimes."

He wanted to laugh now. "Don't tell me. The Hawaiian Poseidon? MacMannan MacLir?"

Another smile. "You're catching on. Who's Mac-Mannan MacLir?"

"Irish version of the same guy. Those sea gods seem to have a pretty tight union, considering the fact that they didn't all get bought out by a bigger god. Pele seems to have knocked all the other fire goddesses off the planet."

"She does have a pretty impressive resumé, you have to admit," Lilly observed, her whole body relaxing against his.

"So I've heard. She sure makes great islands…at least, I think she does. They smell great, I know. And they're warm and windy, which I like. And I think they're colorful, if my poor nearsighted eyes don't deceive me." He lifted a hand up toward the cliffs that towered above them. "Are those trees all flowering?"

She moved a little to look, and Ethan bit back a groan. He would have been much happier if it had been from pain. Unfortunately, it wasn't.

"Some of them are trees. The red blooms are the *'ula,* the gold the gold tree. The white and purple, though, are orchids."

"Orchids?" he asked. "You have orchids growing wild here?"

"Sure," she said with a smile. "It's why they call us a tropical paradise."

"No kidding." He shook his head. "And I used to pay all those bucks for corsages when I was in high school."

"You bought orchids for a high school date?" she demanded.

"No. My mom."

They both went still.

"This memory thing seems to be catching up with me," he mused, unconsciously slipping his free arm around Lilly to hold her against him. "It's only been what, a day, and already I know I like opera, can't see without glasses, know somebody named Sally, and have a mother."

"Who you gave flowers to."

"Yeah."

With a tired face. Sweet, sad, blue eyes. Dingy dresses. He saw her in mountains, too. He wondered why he hated them so much, then.

"You said I have a lot of money, huh?"

"Yep."

He nodded into her hair. "Then when I get back, I'll just buy this valley and visit."

"Visit, huh? You don't want to stay?"

He frowned, again beset by that impatience. "No. I have to go home. I can't stay. But I'll come back and visit when I buy the valley, okay?"

She chuckled against his chest. "Can't."

"Why? Doesn't being a world-famous film star stand for anything anymore?"

"Not unless at least two of your grandparents were Hawaiian, it doesn't. This part of Molokai is all protected by the King Trust. Only people of native descent can buy land here.''

"Okay, fine. I'll buy it for you.''

"Thanks. I already own it. Well, my family does. A little bit, anyway. Enough.''

"Enough? What's enough?''

"Enough to have a little piece of our home that somebody from the outside hasn't stolen.''

"Well, heck. I'm rich. I'll buy the rest back for you.''

"Thanks, Ethan. You're a pal.''

He grinned. "I think so. Where's home?''

"I told you. Here.''

"No. You said you were headed home from here when you found me.''

"Oh. That. Oahu.''

"You don't like it as much as here, huh?''

"Of course I do. Why would you say that?''

"They say if you lose one sense, the rest become more acute. I can hear it in your voice.''

"My family's all on Oahu. My job is on Oahu. So I'm on Oahu.''

"But you'd live here if you could.''

For a second she was quiet. When she answered, he could hear the sigh she tried to hold in. "Yeah. I'd live here.''

"Not many research libraries on Molokai, huh?''

He got another silence. "Not many on Oahu, either.''

He looked down at the top of her head. "Then why stay?''

She didn't even hesitate. "Something will open up.''

"You could probably go anywhere you wanted, Lilly.''

"I don't want to go anywhere, Ethan. I never have.''

He heard it in her voice, but he didn't quite believe it. "You've never been off the islands?"

"Only to go to grad school, but then I came home."

"And that's it?"

A smile again. Patient this time. "Sure. Why not?"

"There's a big world out there," he protested. "All kinds of places to see, people to know."

She shrugged against him. "I guess that makes me a little odd, then. I've never had a desire to meet them."

Ethan didn't know what to say. Surely there was something he could share with her to argue her point. He couldn't remember it, though. And, oddly, he couldn't quite remember an argument stronger than "I've never had a desire to meet them." He'd been lying on this beach for a sum total of a night in a rainstorm, and even with clear evidence of mountains over his head, he could feel a kinship with the place. A slow peace that could almost erase that urge to move.

But not today. Today he needed to go. To be away. To be home, wherever that was, because someone needed him.

His wife? Dulcy, who didn't inspire delight with her memory?

He didn't know. He didn't think so, but that obviously didn't mean much right now.

And so, since he had no answer, he simply lay alongside Lilly, who did inspire delight, and basked in her silence. Her warmth. The lush fullness of her young, strong body in his arms.

"Ethan?"

"Mm-hmm?"

"Are you nearly as sore as I am?"

He chuckled. "Only if by *sore* you mean 'can't move without screaming like a girl.'"

She moved so fast he almost did scream like a girl.

"Okay," he apologized, wincing. "I'm sorry. That wasn't politically correct at all. I meant scream like a chicken."

But she wasn't paying attention. "Oh, my God, Ethan…"

He did his best to flash her an offhand grin. "Did I tell you I can only see out of one eye now?"

It didn't seem to help. "Your face!" she all but wailed.

Her hand was against his cheek again. Ethan tried his best to laugh it off. What he wanted to do was kiss her. Touch her. Rediscover who he was in her arms.

"Lilly, it's okay. I smacked it falling off the boat. Actually, it's not so bad. When I could see with both eyes, there were three of everything and halos everywhere. Now I'm down to doubles."

He couldn't see much, but he thought he caught the glint of tears in those big dark eyes of hers. "It's…oh, Ethan, we have to get you to a doctor. It's your career!"

"It's not that bad."

She didn't answer, which meant that it was. He wondered why it didn't frighten him. If what everybody was telling him was true, his face was his livelihood, and Lilly's stunned reaction was telling him that his best asset was in imminent danger of failing him.

"Lilly," he said, taking hold of her hand. "Believe me when I tell you that I'm perfectly happy to be alive. Everything else will sort itself out."

She opened her mouth and then just shook her head. "You really are a disaster waiting to happen," she protested weakly.

"Now, that seems familiar," he assured her.

She shook her head again and sat all the way up. "You'd think somebody might have mentioned it in one of those millions of interviews people have done with you."

He did his best to grin. "I'm probably much too embarrassed to admit it in public."

Finally, he got her to laugh. "Do you remember if the word *incorrigible* has ever been used in describing you?"

"I wouldn't be surprised."

It wasn't pleasant, but he pushed himself up to a sitting position, as well. His respite was over, his warmth gone. It was time to start getting back, and suddenly he didn't want to do it.

Screw the boat. Screw the kidnapers and the press and the rest of the world. Couldn't he just sneak off into one of those valleys and find out what lay beneath all those buttons and zippers Lilly had belatedly hidden behind? Couldn't he lose himself in that sun-warmed skin? In the deepest, darkest recesses of her, where her passion lay?

God, he wanted to hit something, and he'd only known her a day. Come to think of it, he'd only known himself a day. Maybe this was how Adam felt when he woke up to find that some benevolent being had dropped Eve into his sleeping arms.

Which meant, considering how he felt right now, he didn't blame Adam a bit for following Eve around like a puppy.

Except that his Eve had already said she wouldn't allow it. So he had to revert to a sense of honor he didn't even remember and reestablish his distance.

"Okay," he said, hoping like hell his expression

matched the forced nonchalance in his voice, "what say I break out some breakfast?"

Lilly couldn't seem to answer him. He couldn't tell by looking, but he had the feeling she was still hunched with distress.

"Lilly," he urged, a hand out to her. "It's a beautiful morning, we're alone on a secluded beach on a tropical island. Couldn't we at least pretend we're enjoying it?"

Her laugh was dry. "It would be a heck of a lot easier if I didn't have to look at your face."

He scowled. "Not something I think I've heard often."

She dipped her head. "There's something else."

Ethan recognized reality when he heard it. He didn't let go of her hand, but he didn't pressure her, either.

"All I'm asking is that we can eat some breakfast here, Lilly," he coaxed with what he hoped was an easy smile. "After last night, I think we deserve it."

"After last night we deserve caviar and champagne," she assured him dryly. "It's just...um..."

He squeezed her hand. He wanted to pull her back into his arms. He wanted to court madness with her. He didn't think he was the kind of man who would do that with a wife waiting at home. That didn't seem to matter to his groin, which was in the process of draining every ounce of blood he had left from his head.

"I'm in no condition to take advantage of you, Lilly," he assured her gently, as if he weren't aching like sin.

To his utter astonishment, she laughed. "You're not the one I'm worried about, Ethan."

Ethan damn near stopped breathing altogether. That was absolutely the last thing he needed. So he smiled, as if she hadn't just made everything a hundred times worse.

"They can't take more than a few more hours to find

us, Lilly," he said. "I think both of us are adult enough to last that long."

She just nodded, a lovely brown blur against the white sand, and Ethan didn't want to let her go. But, like the gentleman he hoped like hell he was back in the real world, he let her go so he could retrieve their breakfast.

At which point he finally took note of the waterlogged athletic bag he'd tied to his waist the night before.

"Uh oh."

He had Lilly's immediate attention. "Our supplies..." she protested in a tight voice.

Ethan lifted one side of the torn and tattered bag to lift out a bottle of aspirin and a soggy box of granola bars. He had the feeling that the rest of their supplies were probably littering the beach like driftwood.

"The shoes made it, at least."

"Shoes are the one thing we can probably do without for a few days," Lilly retorted, climbing stiffly to her feet. "The hydrogen peroxide and antibiotic ointment on the other hand..."

Before Ethan could protest, she was on her feet and running around the sheltering foliage toward the roar of the surf. Probably trying to rescue a tube of goo from the sand. Sighing with the serious discomfort he was courting, Ethan struggled to his feet.

"Sit right back down!" she immediately snapped, trotting back toward him with a couple of bottles of mineral water and a jacket in her hands. "No, on second thought, stay there. We can't stay."

"Sure we can," he objected, battling a brief surge of dizziness at his sudden change of altitude. "It's a nice day, I'm hungry, and we have some delicious whole grain clumps to share. I say we just enjoy breakfast."

But Lilly wasn't paying attention to him. Instead she was stuffing her booty back into the athletic bag.

"No breakfast," she said, straightening to take hold of his arm.

Ethan could hardly look up that fast. "Why?"

"The boat. They didn't sink."

He turned toward the water, but he couldn't see more than vague blurs out that far, especially with the sun in his eyes. "We're climbing?" he asked.

Lilly snatched the athletic bag from his hands and reached for him. "We're climbing."

Seven

Ethan didn't move. "There's only one problem."

"What?" Lilly asked, an eye on the boat as it cruised slowly past.

"I can't climb. I'd really like to, Lilly. I mean it. It's just that I think I gave my all during that escape attempt last night. I'm done in."

Lilly stared up at him in disbelief. Well, not really disbelief. One look at that ashen face, that ballooned, purple eye and the various lacerations that had reddened and swelled to ugly gashes told more story than she needed to hear. Lilly was so stiff that when she hefted the athletic bag she thought her arms would fall off, and all she'd done was row an inflatable raft through a few waves. Ethan had collected more injuries than a losing boxer and then done enough calisthenics to exhaust a gymnast. Lilly really couldn't believe he'd made it this far.

But they had to make it farther. She simply couldn't

imagine what would happen if those two men found them again.

"It's not that far," she begged. "Just up the ridge. We can do it."

He smiled as if he hated to disappoint her. "Maybe we can make it in a little while. We can't make it now."

For a minute she just stood there, torn, the bag weighing down her arms and her heart running away with her. Another look out to sea showed nothing but empty water.

"They're still deciding which cove we put into," she said. "Maybe we have some time."

"Atta girl," he agreed, weaving a little on his feet. "If we see them land, we'll run."

Lilly laughed. "You sure have a way with a euphemism."

"It seems to be my life, now, doesn't it?"

Even so, Lilly wasn't satisfied. "We need to at least get back a little farther upstream," she insisted. "That way, if they do land, we'll have time to get going."

"Upstream?" Ethan asked.

Lilly wanted to scream. "You probably can't see it. Come on, Ethan. It's on level ground."

Ethan seemed to be considering something within himself. Finally, though, he sighed and straightened. Then, with deliberate care and no little effort, he took a couple of steps. And sweated. And swayed.

Lilly's feeling of escape was suffering serious erosion. "Come on," she said as if she were simply guiding the way. "Let's walk."

Taking the greatest care as she wrapped her arm around his waist, she turned them inland along the sand toward where she knew the waterfalls were.

It seemed to take hours. The rain forest closed in over and around them, and bright birds flitted through the trees.

Seagulls wheeled and cried overhead, and behind them the surf still assaulted the rocks. But as much as Lilly strained to hear, she didn't detect sounds of approach. Of course, they would have been tough to catch over the rasp of labored breathing and the stutter of stumbling steps.

She wished she could have somehow stayed on that raft. No matter how weary or battered Ethan had been, he could manage as long as he didn't have to rely on that gimpy leg. Now the leg was bleeding a little, probably getting infected. Certainly weak and hurting. Which wasn't the way to get to safety up some pretty steep trails in a morass of mud.

"Don't worry," he offered, as if he heard every worry. "The good guys know where…we are…. They'll be here…soon."

"You mean we have no idea where they are?" Noah said, trying desperately to control his temper.

Poised by the nautical map like a teacher waiting for an algebra answer, the Coast Guard Lieutenant all but flinched. "They're somewhere in the islands," she said. "They have to be."

"And why is that?"

"Because of the proximity of the messages. Because of the last known sighting of the vessel just east of the island of Maui."

"It's not a surfboard you're trying to find here," Noah snapped. "The *Hannah Girl* is quite a good-sized yacht."

Noah wasn't encouraged when the woman gave him what she probably thought passed for a compassionate look. She just looked patronizing. "Unfortunately, Mr. Ross, we have quite a few yachts of that size pass through these waters on a continual basis. Not to mention the ones berthed here."

"You're saying that the combined forces of the Coast Guard, U.S. Navy, FBI and Hawaiian State Police can't find one lousy boat?"

"Noah..." Dulcy warned behind him.

"That's what she's saying," Jack answered.

"My God, you have to do something more than just stand here!" shrilled the thin, elegant blonde beside them.

Noah flinched. Dulcy slipped an arm around the blonde's thin shoulders. "Ellen, they're doing everything they..."

But Ellen wasn't having any of it. Deep-set gray eyes wide with distress, she was trembling and teary and angry. "Oh, *please*. You've been living off him for years! He's given up everything for you, Noah. Everything! And you can't...you can't even..."

Even Noah couldn't argue with her words. "Ellen..."

"You just don't understand," she insisted, her voice harsh. "He has to get back now. He has to come home *now*."

"We'll get him home, Ellen," Dulcy promised, an eye on her distraught husband. "We promise."

Trying his damnedest to hold still, Noah faced the Coast Guard Lieutenant. "Well, what do we do now?"

The Coast Guard Lieutenant shrugged. "You might ask the FBI, but my guess is, you pay the ransom."

"Boy, I can't wait 'til I get my glasses back so I can see all this," Ethan mused, lying on his back at the edge of the stream.

Lilly settled herself down next to him and dropped an armful of something round that rolled into his side. "Want some lunch?"

Ethan looked over. "Where've you been?"

"Trying to get up high enough to keep an eye on our

friends. Lucky for you, there just happened to be quite a few lovely fruit trees along the way. Mango or guava?''

He really paid attention now. ''Really?''

She couldn't help grinning at him. ''Hey, if you have to be running for your life, you sure picked a great place to do it. Almost all the comforts of home.''

Ethan was already wiping one of the mangos off on his shirt hem. ''I think the beds must be softer at home.''

''You can't say you have a waterfall in the bedroom, I bet,'' she challenged, easing down into the cushion of ferns alongside him.

''You're right. I can't. But then, I can't say for sure there's a bed in my bedroom. I can't, in all honesty, say there's a bedroom.''

He was lying with his head propped up on the athletic bag, his rangy frame stretched out before him as if he'd just stopped here on a leisurely walk. If, that is, the walk had entailed a losing fight with a rhino. His face was looking bad, and there was fresh blood along his side and his leg. And his color was about as reassuring as the clouds that were massing along the horizon. The biggest adventure Lilly had ever been on was amid the pages of *Robinson Crusoe,* and here she was trying to recreate it with a battered Man Friday. She just gave up and sat on the ground beside him.

''Y'know,'' he said, wiping the juice from his cheeks with the back of his hand, ''I bet if we just stayed right here, the bad guys wouldn't even see us.''

Lilly chomped down on her own mango, desperately trying not to reach out and clean that little leftover trickle of juice from Ethan's jaw. Geez, a couple of hours away from certain death and she was back to raging hormones. This rescue business was exhausting.

"You need to get to shelter, Ethan," she said again. "It's going to rain."

"I think I could probably make us a shelter. Use vines for lashings, that sort of thing, then top it with palm fronds." He squinted up toward the bit of sky they could see beyond the cliffs. "There are palm fronds around, aren't there?"

"Sure, but what do you plan to use for a radio?"

"I told you. We don't need a radio. I let them know just where we were. We just need to wait."

"For how long?" she asked. "If we stay here, we have no way at all of getting off the island. We have no defense again those two if they show up."

Ethan's eyes were closed. "I'll heave coconuts at 'em."

Lilly watched him, her heart in her throat. "Only if I point you in the right direction."

Never bothering to open his eyes, he grinned sleepily. "See? We make a hell of a team, Lilly."

And then, unbelievably, he fell back to sleep.

They spent the day there. Lilly collected palm fronds and balanced them on driftwood braces to create a kind of lean-to. Ethan made use of his Swiss Army knife to sharpen sticks on which they could split coconuts and braided *hau* fiber into tie-downs. Both of them worked to check out Ethan's growing list of injuries, which now included the completely shut eye and a new slice off his skin along his left ribs from the night before. Lilly dosed Ethan with aspirin and cleaned what she could until she could get Ethan to her store of remedies up at the cabin. The rain rolled in, this time steady, cool and dismal, and the two of them crouched beneath their lean-to and listened for intruders.

By the time the sun disappeared, along with the rain, Lilly knew three very important things. Ethan's friends didn't know where they were, she had to get Ethan to the cabin so they could get help, and he was getting worse instead of better.

"Good thing there's a moon," he murmured, lying on his back with a jacket covering him, his eyes closed.

"You can see it?" Lilly asked from where she sat alongside.

"Nope. I remember it from the other night. But you're kind of glowing, like there's a light shining on you. It's either the moon or I ate the wrong kind of plants today."

Lilly pulled her knees up and wrapped her arms around them. She'd just felt his forehead again, waiting for it to get hot. He was pale and a little sweaty, and his vision was getting worse. His leg was swelling, and his tongue was drying out, despite the water she kept forcing on him. She had to get him up to the cabin, where she could get better help for him than a dwindling bottle of aspirin, and she had to do it before he couldn't make it.

"Ethan..." she began, unable to take her own eyes from the wash of moonlight in his midnight hair.

He didn't open his eyes. "Tomorrow, Lilly."

"Take some more aspirin," she begged.

He smiled. "I already won't dare have a headache for a month. Talk about your mother instead."

Lilly blinked. "My mother?"

"Sure. Don't you have a mother?"

"Well, yes. But why do you want to know about her?"

"I don't suppose you want to hear my line about any mother who gave birth to a woman like you must be worth knowing."

Lilly groaned. "I hope this doesn't mean you're getting your memory back," she threatened. "Because if that's what I get when you really do show up, I'm taking off by myself.''

He was still smiling. ''You wouldn't do that, Lilly.''

''And why not?''

''Because you're the oldest. The oldest never shirks her responsibility.''

She laughed. ''As an only child, just how would you know that?''

A silence. A frown. They'd been playing this kind of game all day. Keeping up innocuous conversations that deliberately wandered into nudges into his past. Not once had he remembered anything.

This time it really seemed to matter. Lilly brushed his hair back off his forehead in a gesture she'd unintentionally learned from her mother. ''I won't leave you here,'' she said. ''I'll take you with me.''

He nodded marginally, his good eye open as if he could really see what she was thinking. ''I know you will, Lilly.''

She didn't know what else to do. It was dark, the temperature was dropping with the ever-present wind, and she was falling in love with a married man.

''Lilly?''

She looked down at him. ''Yes, Ethan.''

''Do I have any kids?''

Suddenly she wanted to cry, too. This was just too much for her. She wanted to be home with her brothers harassing her, her mother comforting her with those callused, caring hands of hers. She wanted to curl up in her Tutu Mary's lap and tell her the truth, that she was suddenly confused and frightened and frustrated, and it had nothing to do with three kidnapers on a boat. That, for the first time in her life, she'd been swamped by the most irrational urge to madness.

''No,'' she assured him, her hand back to his forehead where she knew it shouldn't be as she told him a lie so he could cope. ''You don't.''

He sighed. ''I didn't think so.''

Thank heavens his eyes were closed again. That way he couldn't see the tears that wouldn't dissipate. This was so stupid, Lilly thought. She knew better. She'd known better her whole life, and she'd structured that life to prevent her ever being tempted. Lilly the plain one. Lilly the brain. Lilly who had far too much pragmatism to court dreams of wonder. And here she was tormenting herself with the touch and smell and sound of the very kind of man she'd built those walls to protect herself against.

Pretty girls could expect to see an answering spark in the eyes of a man like this; lovely women with deep, melting eyes and the kind of figure that seemed poured over a perfect frame and set to movement with the wind.

Lilly hadn't been poured. She'd been built. She had eyes no one noticed but her *tutu,* because her *tutu* had the magic, and she had the grace of an earthbound soul. Lilly wasn't of fire, like Pele, but of the earth, like gentle Lono. She was the daughter of Molokai, and she'd known it from her childhood.

And here she was, watching the moon limn a slumbering man and thinking that he would only know her as long as he couldn't see her. Once he could see again, the real Lilly would vanish, the Lilly her *tutu* thought had magic, and Ethan would see only the earth.

And Ethan wasn't the kind of man to settle for the earth when he could court fire.

''Why don't you get some sleep?'' he asked, his voice soft against the steady breath of the wind.

''I probably should.''

He didn't say another word. Just pulled an arm from beneath his marginal covering and opened it for her.

He didn't so much as open his eyes, so that Lilly would know the offer was made without coercion. She was tired, she thought. Bone-tired and frustrated and sad. It couldn't hurt to conserve a little heat the old-fashioned way. After all, it wasn't as if Ethan could manage anything, even if he'd wanted to.

Lilly accepted his invitation and curled up along his right side, so she wouldn't hurt his ribs. She wrapped her own arms around him so he could share her warmth, too, and she closed her eyes against the steady rhythm of his heart. And then she spent the next hour trying so very hard to ignore the warm, hard feel of him.

She'd just begun to relax into a kind of sleep when Ethan stiffened. Lilly opened her eyes to the sight of moon-washed foliage and tumbling water.

"What's..."

She never got the words out. Before she knew what was happening, Ethan was in motion. A finger to her lip, a foot out to the upright that was precariously balancing their hut. A quick roll so that instead of resting on his chest, she lay beneath him. Beneath him and beneath the sudden settle of palm fronds.

"Ethan," she rasped against his shoulder.

"Good news, Lilly," he whispered right into her ear, sending chills chasing through her like lightning. "You didn't kill Louise after all."

And then she heard it. Footsteps. Whispered confrontations. A pair of predators no more than yards away, who had all but stepped on her head in their search for their prey.

"You wanna tell me again what we're supposed to find in the dark?" Louise was demanding.

"It's not dark," Huey assured her. "The moon's out."

"Which makes it a hell of a lot easier to spot people hiding in the bushes. Geez, I think I see 'em right over there. No, there. They're skinny-dippin' in the stream, which is what I wish I was doin'."

"Haven't you done enough time underwater this week?" her cohort asked dryly.

Caught beneath the combined weight of Ethan and their lean-to, Lilly couldn't get enough breath to gasp, much less laugh. But that was what she wanted to do. She wanted to bury her face in Ethan's neck and laugh. She hadn't killed anybody. And the anybody she hadn't killed was still pretty idiotic.

"That wasn't my fault," Louise was whining.

She got an impatient snort. "You Hawaiians were hired because you were supposed to know how to handle stuff like this. I coulda just as well had a couple o' blind monks."

"I told you, you idiot. I'm no more Hawaiian than you are. I'm Italian!"

"Boss said you were Hawaiian."

"Boss also said you knew what the hell you were doin'. Even a damn Italian knows you can't find anything in the dark."

"Then why'd you come?"

"To give that bitch back a little of what she gave me, of course."

"She tried to keep from getting shot," Huey retorted wearily. "Get over it."

That didn't seem to soothe any ruffled feathers. "You try doing that marathon swim in a storm with a big, honkin' hit on the head."

"You keep talking, I'll give you another big honkin' hit on the head."

Now Lilly knew she *was* going to laugh. It was building in her chest, right behind the butterflies bred from Ethan's touch. The fan of his breath against her throat. The exquisite pressure of his body on hers.

Lust or terror or excitement? Lilly's head was spinning and her chest was on fire. Her heart was thundering so loudly she was sure the two hikers could hear it above the waterfall.

"I'm tellin' you," Louise was saying, "you didn't see nothin'. They're not in this cove."

A moment of taut silence, counted by the steady brush of wind through the palms. The gallop of Ethan's heart as it tried to outdistance hers. The almost silent whisper of his breathing.

Lilly was trembling. She wanted to close her eyes, as if that would make it all go away. She couldn't. Ethan couldn't see at all. At least she could make out some movement beyond the palm fronds. She could see the two of them pausing on the path paralleling the stream that thundered from the mountains.

"We need to get back," Louise all but whined. "What if the boss tries to call?"

"If the boss calls, we won't be the ones who have to admit that we lost the paycheck, will we?"

Swish. Rustle. "Well, if you put it that way…"

Lilly heard a sharp sigh and then the brush of sudden movement. "Come on. Let's try later…. You really aren't a Hawaiian? You sure look Hawaiian…."

It seemed that Ethan held Lilly in place for an eternity. She lay perfectly still, straining to hear past the shush of the trees and the chuckle of the water. She did her best to ignore the taut muscles that held her, the glint of one highly amused eye over her. She tried so very hard to deny the melting of her own body's defenses.

Everything was so clear, every sweep of Ethan's eye-lashes, every twitch of movement along his taut jaw. Lilly could feel the sharp edges of his pelvis and the thick force of his thighs. She smelled the salt on his hand where it rested against her cheek and fought the urge to taste it. To just run her tongue along his palm, pull his work-roughened finger into her mouth and suck, like a dessert treat.

It was only Ethan, she thought in deadly rationalization. Only a man I helped off a life raft. A man with no past and an uncertain future. Couldn't I share a little of it with him? Couldn't I, just this once, take a little something for myself?

She betrayed herself with a little sob, and Ethan pulled away.

"Oh, Lilly, I must be crushing you," he whispered, not moving far enough. "You okay?"

Cold. She was cold.

She was ashamed and hungry and seething.

She closed her eyes, so she couldn't see the confusion in his. "Yeah. I'm…uh, fine. How did you ever hear those two?"

For once it was his hand that did the soothing, reaching up to push the hair back from her forehead. "I don't know," he admitted. "Some instinct I honed back in the dark ages, I guess."

Her hair was back, yet his hand still stroked. His body went still. Lilly couldn't open her eyes, couldn't pull away from his touch. He was weaving light through her, heat. He was spinning the moon through her and setting her skin to spangling.

And she couldn't let him.

So she opened her eyes. And promptly fell into the sweet, bottomless blue of his.

Breathing stopped. Movement stopped. Hearts all but stopped.

Kiss me, she wanted to beg. *Touch me with those workman's hands of yours.*

She held perfectly still, captured by motionless hands and the dark night of his eyes. She ached and sweated and called on every ancestor, every god, every old magic she could to keep her honor.

But nobody listened.

His lips were soft. Ah, so soft, like the earth, like settling into the warm, dark soil when the sun heated it. His hands were roughened and tender, hesitant leaves fluttering against her eyes in a breeze. His body was solid, hard as rock, a fortress against loneliness, and Lilly wanted to fold herself into it and rest. She wanted to climb it and fly. She wanted to span it and live.

Her heart thundered, and her skin shimmered. Her hands sought him out like a blessing, and she sobbed again, her heart exploding like fireworks. Like deadly missiles that shattered sense.

That quickly, he pulled away. Gasping, cursing, his forehead against hers. His hands still. His lips suddenly too far away for Lilly to survive.

"I'm...I'm sorry...." he whispered, his voice as pale as his skin. "Oh, Lilly, I'm so sorry."

But Lilly, who finally knew what the magic was that she'd missed all these years, could only smile. "I guess we're not as adult as we thought, huh?"

Eight

Ethan knew he was in good shape, because this climb hadn't killed him yet.

''I don't think…they'll find…us….'' he protested yet again.

''Neither will your friends,'' Lilly answered, just as she had before. Then she pulled him back to his feet and turned him uphill, where his feet would get sucked into ankle-deep mud and the midges would torment his hot, prickly skin. His left leg was completely numb, and his head was pounding like the surf. And he was sure they were only a couple of hundred feet higher than when they'd started about eighty hours ago.

He'd known when he lost control the night before that he would have to pay for it. He just hadn't thought he would pay *before* he died.

''Have some more water,'' Lilly urged somewhere near his pounding head.

"No thanks."

But God, it had been good. It had felt so right, as if, after wandering forever, he'd finally found the other half of himself. Even not knowing where he'd searched, or what he'd gone through to get there, he knew. As deep as breathing and blinking, as old as his bones. Lilly hadn't just felt soft and warm and alive in his arms. She'd felt right.

Which was probably a good thing, because, married or not, Ethan had a feeling that was the last time in his life he was going to get to kiss a woman.

"Lilly," Ethan gasped after another hour. "This isn't going to work."

"Yes, it is," Lilly insisted, resettling her arm around his waist. "We can do this."

He stumbled and stopped, his free hand out to thin air, his face ashen. "Not when you're...squeezing our broken ribs, we can't," he managed.

Lilly almost let go on the spot. "I'm sorry," she told him. "But we have to move, Ethan. We can't let them catch us again. I don't think they're going to chance letting us escape a third time."

He nodded, his breathing ragged, his face all but unrecognizable from the swelling. "I know...but you didn't...tell me...Hawaiians were...mountain...goats...."

Lilly wanted to cry. She wanted to be able to just tuck him under a tree where he could rest. She was terrified she was asking too much of him, and yet she knew that the kidnapers would find their trail at any time. The only way to escape them was to use trails only a native knew. And natives knew steep trails.

"It's not that much farther," she lied. "I promise."

Even as miserable as he looked, he grinned down at her. "Nice try. Did I tell you I'm afraid of heights?"

Lilly took a considered look over the edge of the trail. "Then I guess it's a good thing you can't look down. Did I tell you there's a lovely, cool pool of water near the cabin?"

"That's nice. Did I tell you I'm not going to live long enough to see it?"

Distant voices drifted up to them on the wind. Lilly turned, but the dense foliage kept her from seeing the beach. She'd tried to take a few minutes to hide the evidence of their presence, but she was afraid it hadn't worked. Which meant there was only one choice.

"Come on, Mr. Superstar Hero," she urged in a dry voice. "Let's do the impossible."

And it *was* impossible. The rain had turned the red earth into a slick, deadly morass. The sides of the valley were precipitous. Now that they were away from the beach, the wind had died, leaving behind a sticky, hot humidity that sapped energy and breath. Even Lilly, who trekked these mountains at least every other week, was exhausted. She couldn't imagine what Ethan was going through.

"Just a ways farther," she urged, shifting to take more of his weight. "Please."

Gasping, mouth open, he just nodded.

"Remember," she said, not knowing what else to do, how to keep them both on their feet, "I have home-field advantage. I can hide from them forever."

"Then let's…hide.…"

"The radio," she said like a chant. A prayer, actually. "That'll bring help in minutes. We need to get to the radio."

She looked up and saw how far they had to go and

despaired. And kept slogging along, the mud to her ankles, the earth sucking at her shoes, the dense vegetation closing in on her like a thousand hands, the heat sucking out her air and plastering her hair to her neck.

Well, she thought dismally, at least the fight for survival was taking all her time and attention. It was better than regretting what had happened the night before. What had almost happened. What she wished with all her heart had happened, even knowing she would have roasted in hell for it.

But at least if she was going to die on a cliffside on Molokai, she would go with the memory of that one perfect kiss to see her off.

"What do you mean, you can't find him?"

The short kidnaper Ethan had nicknamed Huey stood hunched over the cellphone as if waiting for a physical blow. "He got away again."

"Again."

Huey had hoped he wouldn't have to have this conversation with the boss. He'd especially hoped he wouldn't have to have it with his cohorts standing by. They were all looking stupid enough as it was without him having to admit to it.

"Somehow he disabled the ship and got off. We're looking all over the island for him, but we haven't found him yet. But don't worry. This island's only so big."

"It is, on the other hand, very tall," the boss said in clipped tones.

"Which only helps us. Tough for a guy to climb that high with a coupla bullets in him."

It didn't take the prolonged silence on the other end of the phone to make Huey immediately regret that admission, either.

"Bullets?" the boss finally asked, voice harsh and low. "You *shot* our meal ticket?"

"Well…we didn't mean to. He must've moved."

Another silence, this one long enough to make Huey sweat.

"He also, I understand, has help."

Huey flinched. "How did you know?"

"Reports have come in that a young woman has gone missing in your area. Expected home from a trip to Molokai yesterday. I imagine you were going to tell me about it."

"Well, yeah. Sure. Once we got them both."

"We're running out of time, you know. That false sighting of Ross's boat east of the Big Island is only going to help us for so long. Even now the search and rescue people are widening the grid. And to add to the problem, there have been some…unexpected developments that have to be dealt with."

Huey wasn't sure whether the boss meant *his* unexpected developments or something more. "Uh, unexpected developments?" he asked, expecting a blast of fury.

When he got only another silence, he felt even worse. He felt worse enough for a stomach pump.

"This guy really looks like Cameron Ross, huh?" the boss asked.

Huey looked at the phone as if it had changed into a snake. "Well, who the hell else should he look like?"

"As a matter of fact, he might just look like Cameron Ross's cousin. Ethan Campbell."

It took Huey a full minute to answer. Didn't it just figure, the way this operation was going? Italians he'd thought were Hawaiians, movie stars who could work computers, and now this. "You mean, you had us kidnap the wrong guy?"

"I mean nobody on the damn planet knew he wasn't Cameron Ross except Cameron Ross, idiot. They switch places sometimes."

"Like those twins in *Parent Trap,* huh?"

Huey didn't think the boss needed to use words like that.

"Well, what do we do?" he asked to interrupt.

"We catch him, of course. We get the ransom, just like we'd planned, since Mr. Ross—or whatever the hell his name is—feels particularly guilty about his cousin getting kidnaped. And then we make damn sure that cousin *and* that girl who's with him end up too dead to tell anybody who snatched them."

"Oh." Finally Huey felt better. He always did work better with a plan. Besides, he only had one lousy island to search. How difficult could that be? Even with Italians for Hawaiians. "Okay."

Lilly didn't know whether to laugh, sing or cry. They'd made it. Heaving and sweating and filthy, but it didn't matter. She could hear the tumble of the waterfall that cascaded from the cliff to her left, and smell the ginger and frangipani her aunts had planted by the cabin to counteract all the "guy smells." She knew she was home the same way her ancestors had recognized stars, only she recognized fern and leaf and bird. The smell of the earth and the growl of the water. The touch of the high breeze on her perspiration-soaked face. Even if she hadn't been running for her life, she would have been glad.

"You still with me?" she asked, hitching up her hold on Ethan a little.

"We there yet, Mom?"

Lilly couldn't help a chuckle. He'd been asking that same thing for three hours, like a four-year-old watching for Disneyland from the back seat of a sedan.

"We're here. Can't you hear the swimming pool being filled?"

There was a pause as he worked to put one foot in front of the other. "I can hear my bronchi screaming. Do me a favor and look down to see if my leg is still there. I have the most awful feeling I left it back on that mountain somewhere."

"It's right here," she said. "I promise. And it's going to start feeling better soon. I store a lot of herbal remedies up here in the cabin. We're up near one of the temples for the *kahuna lapa'au la'au.*"

"Of course. It all becomes clear to me."

Lilly grinned. "The medical *kahunas.* Like my ancestors."

He managed a nod. "A noble profession. One I truly appreciate right now."

"You'll appreciate it even more when we get you horizontal. Now hold on."

The porch of the cabin had rotted away years ago, so that the roof supports grew from the ground. The construction was iffy, the windows almost wider than the walls, the one-room building designed for shelter rather than ostentation.

Shelter they had. Ostentation they didn't. The bed was iron and badly sprung, the furniture handcrafted by old Uncle Kilo, who couldn't square anything to save his life, and the decor early rutting boar.

But there was food inside, and liquor, and herbs drying from the ceiling. The breeze would sail through the rolled-up blinds to refresh Ethan, and the silence would soothe him. And the radio in the corner of the room would call for help.

One hand clamped around the waistband of Ethan's trousers, Lilly gave the front door the good shove it needed to open past the swell of humidity. She tossed the half-full gym bag onto the floor and then focused on getting Ethan in after it.

"Lift your left leg."

"Can't."

So she lifted it. Then she braced the almost useless appendage against her own thigh as she got Ethan to swing his right leg up into the room.

"See how easy that was?"

She was literally shoving his left foot forward and bracing it against her leg. After the hauling Lilly had done on the waist of those trousers, nobody was ever again going to mistake them for tailored. Ethan's soft linen shirt hung limp and soaked against his skin, and his hair curled against his glistening forehead. His eyes were half-closed and his breathing a continuous grunt from the pressure she had to exert on his sore ribs to keep him upright.

But they were there. He would be safe now. He would be better.

He would be taken away from her to recover with his wife.

Lilly would have sworn simple guilt wouldn't make her stumble, but stumble she did, inches from getting Ethan onto the bed. She tangled her feet up against his useless one and sent them both pitching headlong.

Thank God for iron. The bed screamed only a little louder than Ethan when they both hit the mattress. But it held. And Lilly found herself chest to chest with a suddenly wide-eyed Ethan.

"I promised horizontal," she gasped with a grin.

She was scrabbling back off the bed by the time he got any breath to answer.

"I probably...deserved that."

Lilly should have been dusting herself off. She should have been raising blinds and calling for help. Instead she carefully got Ethan situated so that he was all facing one way. Then, because she couldn't help it, she pushed that damp, thick hair back off his forehead.

"Don't be an ass," she said, then grinned again. "Besides, any penance incurred for a certain spontaneous insanity in which I also participated last night was paid up about two hours ago on the trail. Now, take another rest while I get some stuff together."

He closed his eyes. "I want to soak in that pool," he all but whined like a fractious child.

Lilly was still grinning. "Later. After you can get your leg to move again."

Humming *La donna è mobile,* she went about re-opening the cabin she'd recently closed. The wind rustled in, and the light bathed them and Lilly refilled the water jugs from the pool of water that was both play area and shower. She checked the Coleman lanterns for fuel, the shelves for canned food and the surrounding hillside for guava, breadfruit and bananas. And then, her hair pulled back with a strip of white cloth and her oversized shorts traded in for the flowered *mu'umu'u* she kept at the cabin, she gathered her herbs to treat Ethan's wounds. *Kaoli* vine for his broken ribs, *'ulei* and *koa* for his lacerations. *Awa* tea and *awapuhi* for his head, and *popolo* in case of infection. All collected with loving hands and chanted blessings from the precipitous side of the mountaintop where the *kahuna lapa'au la'au* had planted and then cultivated them with such care over the centuries.

"It is a *heiau*, little Lilly," her Tutu Mary had said,

holding her tiny hand as they'd stood high on the mountain, with the sun filtering through those towering trees to dapple them with blessed warmth. "A temple. Can you feel the *mana?* The power? Can you see that the plants used to treat the most minor illnesses are planted close to the top where they are easiest to harvest? A *kahuna lapa'au la'au* must risk more, the more serious the illness she treats. This power is not an easy one, this way not frivolous. This way is so sacred that none are left who have the right to call themselves *kahuna.* Too many of the secrets are lost, my little Lilly Malama. But the gifts wait here, just where they were left, for a special person to rediscover them."

A special person like Lilly, whose middle name meant "caring." But Lilly had only walked those high paths with her Tutu Mary. And when she'd had the chance to rediscover the magic, she'd run away to Kansas instead.

She'd run because standing in that dappled sunlight all those years ago, she *had* felt the mana. She'd heard old whispers, seen shadows she'd never been able to explain. She'd heard the place call to her like a siren luring her off a cliff, and it had frightened her.

It still frightened her. But at least now she'd come to the compromise of using her skills to search out some of the old ways. At least, even if only in books, she was being reintroduced to her mother's ancestors. And maybe soon she would feel better about taking Tutu Mary's gnarled old hand back in hers and walking to the edge of that old precipice.

"What were you chanting just now?"

Startled by the sound of Ethan's voice, Lilly looked up from where she was preparing her pastes and bandages to see to his leg.

"Oh, I'm sorry," she apologized. "I didn't mean to wake you up."

His smile was soft and sleepy. "You didn't. It did take me a minute to remember where I was when I saw you, though. Is that a dress?"

"*Mu'umu'u*. It's a little more comfortable than trying to downsize your shorts."

"Prettier, too, I bet."

Lilly took a look down at the faded crimson and blue flowers scattered over the shapeless material and smiled. "Whatever else you might be, Ethan," she said, "you're definitely an optimist."

"Does the music go with the dress? You've definitely moved on from *La donna è mobile*."

Lilly dipped her head in chagrin, caught like a child betraying personal secrets. "It was a blessing," she said. "For healing."

She all but flinched, only to have Ethan reach a hand out to hers. "It's beautiful."

She still couldn't look up. "I, uh, have some herbal remedies that might help. But we're going to have to dispense with your pants again."

"Why don't we just cut 'em?" he asked. "I doubt we're expected at anything dressy soon, are we?"

"No." She tried to flash a smile, but failed. "Of course not."

"Lilly."

She'd been about to get to her feet. Just his voice brought her back down.

"You've seen my butt before, Lil," he said. "So that can't be what's making you so uncomfortable. What is it?"

Lilly almost laughed. What was it? "In twenty-five words or less?" she asked, trying hard to be flippant.

"In however many words you want."

"What could be the matter?" she demanded, fighting for levity. "Like you said—it's a beautiful day, we're in paradise and we have all the fresh fruit and *poi* we can eat. Of course, we also have kidnapers after us, you look like a train wreck, and I've already missed two days of work, which isn't going to go over well with the boss. Tough to do without the third hula girl from the end, you know...."

She tried hard to pull her hand away, but Ethan wouldn't let her. "You're not really a hula girl."

Lilly tugged, to no avail. "Oh, but I am. Six days a week for every camera-toting tourist on Waikiki. It's what research librarians with no library do here. Of course, I only work with a strictly traditional troupe, which is good, because I don't have to wear a blue tinsel skirt or be a Polynesian goddess."

"You just have to offer up sacred music for people with videocams and polyester shirts."

She was going to pull away now. She meant to. "This isn't the time to be arguing the merits of tourism versus the protection of dignity."

"But this place makes you sad, and I thought you loved it here. And I imagine it has to do with those tourists."

Lilly did manage to disengage her hand this time and got to her feet. Ethan with his faulty memory and clouded eyes still caught too much. So she hid. She stood away from him where she could look out the window.

The sun was lower now, golden against the shuddering leaves of palm and *koa* and *pau*. In the distance Lilly could see the shimmer of it against the flat expanse of ocean. She could hear the stream that spilled off mountains that climbed another thousand feet to their cloud-wreathed summits. She could smell the ginger and plumeria and eucalyptus, and she could see the gulls and petrels and shearwaters that spun and soared near the water.

Home. She was home. She was tucked against her mountains like a baby to a mother's warmth, and she never wanted to move. And yet, she was so afraid of this place, of those old shadows and whispers at the edge of the mountain, that she faced those vacant smiles and smug preconceptions almost every day of her life.

"I guess I'm kind of caught," she said quietly, almost to herself. "My Tutu Mary says I have the old magic. The *mana* of a *kahuna*. She wants me to devote myself to rediscovering all the secrets that live up at the top of this mountain."

"Is that so bad?"

Lilly laughed. "It is if you want to have a social life. If you want to live in the twentieth century. I'm afraid I'm not like the crowd on Niihua, who prefer the ways of their ancestors. I like computers. I like microwaves and washing machines. But I don't seem to want to pay the dues for having them."

"Dues being grass skirts and tiki lights?"

Lilly shrugged and closed her eyes, more honest here than any place on earth. "What I truly want is to bring the technology here without sacrificing anything for it. But to bring those things here, to this mountain, seems like sacrilege. So I commute back and forth, like a time traveler. And I can't settle in either place anymore. I also find that I need to make a living at something, which is damn tough to do on an island with fewer people than the average hotel on Waikiki."

"What about your family?" he asked.

Lilly actually chuckled. "My family," she said and smiled again. "My grandmother Chang sets extra plates for the ancestors on New Year's, and my grandfather Rodriguez attends mass every morning, rain or shine. My mother, Tutu Mary's daughter, thinks the whole Hawaiian cultural revival is silly. My sister was runner-up for Miss Hawaii and now reports the weather on Channel Twelve in a grass skirt. My three brothers are all playing football for scholarships so they can be, respectively, a banker, CPA and computer genius. My father—Michael Chang Kokoa—retired from the Navy SEALs last year. His feeling is that Hawaii was invented to house the U.S. military. His father, Tommy Kokoa, drank himself to death when my dad was ten. He was a great surfer, though, from all accounts.''

''And your Tutu Mary?''

Lilly lifted her eyes back to the sky. ''Lives about three mountain ridges over with the graves of the rest of her family.''

She heard Ethan go very still. ''She has leprosy?''

''My mother spent her childhood being checked for lesions. Her memory of Hawaiian history is probably a little more tainted than others', which might just explain her aversion to revisiting it.''

''Which makes you the throwback.''

Lilly turned on him. ''The what?''

He didn't seem upset or amused by her recitation. He shrugged. ''A genetic throwback. You hear older voices. The magic your grandmother talks about.''

Lilly was having trouble breathing. ''How do you know?''

His smile was soft. ''You'll catch the Scots and Irish throwing a few of those up every generation. Seems to be an island thing, I guess.''

''Then you're Irish?''

''Sure....'' Another smile, this time chagrined. ''Irish

or Scottish, I think. Maybe both. Land seems to be in our blood. The sacrilege isn't what you bring to the land, it's giving the land away.''

Lilly shook her head. ''That may just be the song of the dispossessed,'' she said. ''Think of how little of Hawaii the natives own anymore.''

''Are you so afraid of that old magic?'' he unaccountably asked.

And Lilly had to tell him the truth. ''Yes. Even the people who are really interested in resurrecting the culture don't seem to hear what I do…see what I do.''

''Doesn't necessarily make you crazy,'' he said gently. ''Might make your grandmother right.''

Lilly didn't know whether to laugh or cry. How could a rich *haole* understand her better than her family? How come he had to already be married?

''She'll be happy to hear that,'' Lilly said, rubbing her suddenly damp palms against her thighs and stepping away from her view of paradise. ''Now, let's get your pants off, big boy.''

''Did you already call for help?'' Ethan asked.

''Once I get you taken care of.''

Once she'd given herself just a few last moments alone with him. After placing that call, she would have no more than another hour before her uncles made it over the mountain. And then Ethan would be gone from her, from this mountain, forever. So she'd stalled. She'd picked her herbs and prepared her salves and watched Ethan sleep as if she had a real hold over him, and she'd put off making that call for just a few more minutes.

''I wanted to get these plants in before dark,'' she lied. ''I also think we need to get something on those injuries. They've spent the day in all kinds of mud and goo, you know.''

She wasn't sure whether she should feel better or worse that Ethan couldn't seem to argue the point. "Can I take a dip in that mountain pool?"

How could one smile dispel every ghost on the mountain? Lilly saw it, teeth and eyes and outrageous dimple, and could have withstood them all. But there, deep in that myopic blue, she saw the understanding. The empathy. The old ghosts she had a feeling walked somewhere through Ethan's memory. And so, once again, even more dangerously than before, she courted sin.

She didn't kiss him. She didn't fling her clothes off and take advantage of their isolation and need. She simply smiled back and ignored that radio a little while longer.

They played in the pool like children, stripping away the fears and frustrations and insanities like old clothes, and then, soaking and sated, Lilly helped Ethan back to bed, where she hummed and chanted quietly to herself as she wrapped him in old herbs and kind wishes. And then, as the sun set again into a trembling ocean, she turned from his sleeping form to finally call for the help that would take him away from her.

Which all might have been well and good, except for one thing. When Lilly went to fire up the radio, it wouldn't turn on.

Nine

The first thing Lilly did was light the lanterns. The second was to spend a moment roundly cursing the meticulous lack of care her uncles kept of the radio. She probably could have spent a moment chastising herself, since she'd been the last in a long line of people to ignore the only evidence of the twentieth century to grace the cabin. But it wouldn't have served.

She knew what the problem probably was. Well, two of the problems it could be. A bad battery or the effects of humidity on connections or wires. Or all of the above.

Even without a memory, Ethan probably could have taken one look at the damn thing and fixed it with a bobby pin and a banana peel. But when Lilly thought to look over at him, it was to find him already asleep.

No surprise. She should have been surprised he was still breathing. Even with the aloe vera and compresses on his face, it still looked battered and sore. She had ti leaves wrapping his leg and his chest, where her medicines were trying to counteract some of his abuse, and his clothes were still soaked and wrinkled. One eggplant linen shirt, with sleeves ripped off and top three buttons missing. One pair of custom-tailored slacks hacked off above the knee. Bare, blistered feet and damp curling hair.

He looked like a mugging victim. She hurt at how hard it was to look away.

How could this happen? How could she, the practical, earthbound Lilly Malama Kokoa, have fallen so completely in love in so short a time? How could she be so stupid? So shortsighted? So whimsical?

If Lilly had heard this story about another woman falling in love with the man known to the world as Cameron Ross, she would have nodded sagely and said, "Well, of course. Who wouldn't fall in love with the most handsome man on screen? Especially if she's as plain looking as that."

But Ethan wasn't Cameron Ross. Lilly wasn't sure what that meant. Maybe he had simply perfected having two personalities. Maybe he was a different person without all those memories that defined the man who had charmed millions with his lazy, sexy smile and sophisticated banter. Lilly didn't know. She did know that when she looked at Ethan, she no longer saw the ghost of Cameron Ross superimposed over his features. She saw someone smaller, quieter, more human. Someone completely at odds with his reputation.

She saw just Ethan, the man she'd pulled from a life raft and had an adventure with.

The man she'd already, in the space of forty-eight hours or so, fallen in love with.

The man she wasn't sure she wouldn't trade in her honor for.

Knowing that he would never ask her to do that only made her love him more.

So, she decided, wiping surprise tears from the corners of her eyes, she had to do the right thing. She had to get him back to his wife and the child she carried. She had to walk away from him as if this all had meant nothing and go back to her life.

Maybe, she thought, as she sat down to take apart the radio, after all this was over, she would spend a week or so on Kalaupapa with Tutu Mary and talk about those old shadows. Maybe she should ask if it was okay to cook in a microwave and chant with old ghosts on a mountainside.

The Coast Guard Lieutenant who had given Noah Campbell the bad news about his cousin was named Betty Williams, and she was worried. She'd just finished going over the latest reports from the search and rescue teams, and was sharing them with the FBI liaison.

"Come on," he was saying, raking an impatient hand over his gray crewcut. "This isn't L.A. How hard can it be to find him?"

Betty handed over the reports with a shrug. "There's a lot of area to hide in," she said. "Not just water, but land. And trust me—it's easier to find somebody by chopper in Los Angeles than in the islands of Hawaii."

The agent tore apart his hair a little more. "Yeah, I know. It just would have been so much easier to blindside 'em."

"You're finally handing off the ransom?"

"There's a team going out now. We can't put it off any longer, hoping to find him."

Betty, a trim, precise woman with a blond braid and businesslike hazel eyes, considered the FBI agent carefully. "You really think you're going to get him back once the ransom is paid?"

The agent looked over his shoulder like a teenager in a cemetery. Cameron Ross was in the next room, and he didn't need to hear the bad news. "The truth?" he asked. "We've had the story out on the airwaves all day. The longer we go without so much as a suspected sighting, the less our chances are of a positive outcome."

"But you're watching the drop point."

"Like hawks."

She nodded, stretched and sighed. "Well, I'd be more than happy to stay around and help, but now that the word is officially out who we're dealing with here, the big boys have shown up to take over. Not that I mind. I don't want to be the one telling the news crews that we let Cameron Ross's favorite cousin get kidnaped and killed out here."

The agent, a fatherly type who'd seen a quiet transition into retirement blasted to hell in the past few days, just smiled. "It's why they pay us big boys the big bucks," he said.

Betty smiled back. "In that case, I'll just have to get my big bucks some other way. Good night, Tom."

"Good night, Betty."

Tom watched Betty walk on out, thinking nothing more than how nice a uniform could look on a woman. Then, heaving his own sigh, he walked back to update Cameron Ross.

Ethan wasn't sure what woke him. Maybe the sunlight, or the birdcalls outside the window. Maybe the freshening breeze across his face. He did know that he felt better. He still ached like a sore tooth, but at least he was sure all his parts were in working order, and his head didn't feel as if it were being used as a gong.

His eyes hadn't improved any. He realized that when he opened them to discover no more than geometrics again, this time bamboo and sky and what he had a feeling was unpainted tin. When he tested his memory, it was to find that it hadn't made a miraculous comeback, either. Whatever or whoever he'd been before waking up in that lifeboat was still lost back in that cotton wool he seemed to hit every time he went searching for something familiar.

As far as he could prove it, he, Ethan somebody, had only existed on this earth for a few brief snatches of time before waking up barefoot and tuxedoed on a life raft. He had been in some mountains once. Not these. Greener, softer, older. Harsher. He had had a mother, which meant he should have some kind of family to remember. He didn't. He remembered a Sally with flour-dusted hands and a big, blond smile. He remembered tiny, fierce Dulcy standing in yet other mountains. Rugged, sparse, aspen-hued. Mountains he still preferred not to visit.

Then why did he feel so happy in these? What old voices did he hear here that seemed so comfortable? What old gods must he have known?

Or was it as simple as the fact that Lilly belonged to these mountains? Lilly, just as lush, just as fertile and sweet. Lilly, as nourishing and nurturing. Try as he might, he couldn't imagine walking away from the smell of frangipani and jasmine, from the sound of kestrels and gulls, from the feel of warm, humid wind.

From the molasses-thick comfort of Lilly's voice.

It would have been so much easier if he'd just dallied with a little lust. After all, if he were a normal guy back beyond that wall of anonymity, wouldn't he have had to be dead not to respond to Lilly's shape and voice and smell? Wouldn't he have wanted to test the contours of her face with his fingers as well as his eyes?

But Ethan was very much afraid that somehow he'd careened right past that off-ramp on the disaster highway. Somewhere between the moment he'd first heard her laugh out on the ocean beneath the ludicrous orange and yellow of her sail, and the moment he'd woken up this morning wrapped in herbs and old blessings, he'd fallen in love.

Head over proverbial heels.

He waited to hear her voice. He turned his head when he smelled her fragrance. He wanted to make her laugh and smile. He wanted, oh, he wanted, to make her cry out in surprise at the passion he could provoke in her.

But he wasn't the man to do it. And so he had to eke out their remaining moments together until the rest of the world descended on them and pulled them irrevocably apart.

Which was when it finally occurred to him that he was looking up into a sunlit sky.

The last thing he remembered, it had been dusk, and Lilly had been walking over to fire up the radio. If that was so, why were they still here?

He looked over to the far corner of the cabin, to see that the radio still sat there. But Lilly didn't. She wasn't anywhere in the cabin.

Ethan didn't think he was the kind of person to panic, but he felt it now, sudden and sharp in his chest. If anything had happened to her...

He'd made it to his feet when the door opened and Lilly walked in.

"Oh," she said, wiping her hands on something. "You're up. How do you feel?"

Her hair was down, drifting like lavaflow over a bright

profusion of what must have been flowers. Ethan blinked, suddenly wishing like hell he could pull her into focus. Wanting at least a few minutes of crystal-clear Lilly before giving her away.

But he knew perfectly well that having that much of her would make it that much harder to do, so he grinned with what he hoped was world-class nonchalance.

"I was afraid you'd gone off and left me for a younger movie star," he said.

"I tried." She was smiling, he thought, but her voice was tight and small. "But no matter where I looked, all I could find were older movie stars. You ready for breakfast?"

"I don't know. We having it here or down at the police station?"

At that, some of the stiffness seemed to leave her, and it looked like she sagged. In that moment Ethan finally took stock of the shapes in the room to realize that there was only one bed, and he'd been in it.

"Lilly, damn it," he snapped, taking a tentative step toward her. "You should have kicked me out of bed. I've certainly done my share of sleeping on the ground."

"Stop it, Ethan," she retorted softly. "I was perfectly happy. Well, except for the fact that I couldn't quite get the radio to work, which means we may be stuck here a little longer than we thought."

He would have been a liar to say he didn't experience just a moment of relief. Just the tiniest flash of guilty delight.

"Anything I can do?"

"You know anything about radios?"

He shrugged. "Hell, who knows? How does it work?"

Lilly turned toward the biggest shape in the corner, gray and stacked, like boxes on end. "It's battery-operated, since we don't have electricity up here. I've changed the battery and tried to clean off any rust from the connectors and stuff. But…'' He thought she lifted her hands in a classic sign of helplessness. "I've been trying to decide if I can leave you alone long enough to get over the rest of the mountain and down to civilization on the other side. I saw the boat again this morning, but I don't know if they're back in this valley or not."

Ethan limped over to what must have been the radio and examined it. "Any spare parts?"

"A whole box full."

"Then let's start testing parts."

There were two units, one a regular long-wave for weather and news, the other a short-wave. Neither, it seemed, had received much attention over the years. Within twenty minutes Ethan had elicited visual reports from Lilly that reinforced his belief that what wasn't rusted was worn-out. He would attempt to replace what was needed, but he thought she might just have to make that trek.

"…and this is the news at the top of the hour…

"We're getting someplace!" Lilly crowed.

"Still can't call out," Ethan told her.

"There's something reassuring about hearing another voice sometimes, though," she admitted, turning up the sound level on the old radio as Ethan felt his way through the other set.

"No new developments on the bizarre plot to kidnap Cameron Ross," the radio announcer intoned.

Ethan froze.

Lilly gasped. "My God…"

Ethan put a quieting hand on her arm. His heart was suddenly racing.

His past. All here. Invading the bubble of their isolation like a stain on a pristine shore.

"The reports first came in on Wednesday that Cameron Ross's yacht, the *Hannah Girl,* had been reported missing east of the island of Hawaii, with Mr. Ross on board. But yesterday afternoon the FBI announced that Mr. Ross was not, after all, lost at sea. A kidnaping plot has been un-covered with Mr. Ross as its target. Not only that, but the wrong man was kidnaped."

Ethan looked at Lilly, but she couldn't seem to look away from the radio.

"I'd like to make a personal plea to the kidnapers," a new voice announced. A voice so like his own that Ethan felt disoriented. "They have, by mistake, taken my cousin, Ethan Campbell...."

Ethan was sure he said something else, this man with his own voice. He never heard it. He only heard Lilly's gasping surprise.

"You're not him!"

Ethan could only shake his head. Another Cameron Ross. Another man with his face and voice. A shadow second self that shared so much of what he was. Ethan struggled to remember more, to pull up that other Cam-eron. That second self who had stood in the mountains with him, who would know what Pea Ridge, Virginia, meant. Who would remember his mother and the orchids and a hundred other things Ethan couldn't.

Who could explain why he wanted to laugh and cry at the same time.

"You were right," Lilly was saying, wonder in her voice. "You kept saying you weren't Cameron Ross. We didn't believe you!"

Her hand was on his arm. That calming, comforting hand. Ethan felt as if he were going to explode. He felt suddenly cast adrift, spun around, left again shoeless and senseless in a life raft with no landmarks to steer by.

Except for that soft, soothing hand. Except for that seductive smell of plumeria and jasmine.

Except for Lilly.

He took hold of that hand in his. "Lilly..."

She was so close he should have seen into her eyes. He just knew they were wide, afraid, excited. "You remember?"

"No...no, I don't...."

Because she was Lilly, she didn't hesitate. She just knelt before him and pulled him into her arms. "You will, though," she promised. "The minute you get back and see your cousin."

Ethan closed his eyes against the sweet sin of her hair. The lush warmth of her body. He wrapped his own arms around her and drew her close, wrapped himself around her, as if he could brace his confusion against her. As if he could once again lose that outside world in her arms.

"My cousin..." he muttered, only able to shake his head.

Somehow, he didn't think that should provoke laughter. But Lilly was chuckling against him. Ethan leaned back, as if he could gauge her expression. "You going to share with the class?"

She was smiling. He could see those strong white teeth as she lifted a hand to stroke his face. "You've been dragging me along on this disaster under false pretenses."

"I have?"

"Why, yes. You're no film star at all."

Ethan captured her hand against his cheek and held it there, the only warmth he could find on a tropical island. "I think I told you that."

"Yeah, but nobody believed you. You know perfectly

well I only rescued you from that life raft because I
thought you were a world-famous sex symbol. Now I find
you're just a—''

''Businessman.''

Wider smile. A bubble of exhilaration in his own chest.

''See?'' she chuckled again. ''That wasn't so hard, was
it? What kind of business?''

''I don't know.'' He could hardly breathe. Her hand on
his skin. Her face so close he could touch it. ''I don't
care.''

He did touch it. He reached out his free hand as if
reaching for balance and found her face. Her soft face,
her smile-crinkled face that seemed to freeze at his touch.
Her dear, familiar, fascinating face that he wanted so
badly to see.

''Ethan...''

Her voice sounded so hurt. So tense. She tried to pull
her hand back, as if calling back her own compassion.
But Ethan wouldn't have it. He caught that hand tight and
turned it toward his lips. And he tasted her palm. Her
fingers. Her wrist. He felt the pulse jump beneath his
mouth and smelled the sudden tang of salt in her sweat.

He could taste her excitement.

''Ethan, please...''

''Now *you're* forgetting,'' he accused, sweeping his fingers along her cheek, outlining the shell of her ear, seeking the long column of her throat.

She could barely seem to form words. ''What? What
am I...oh...forgetting?''

He let go of her hand, only to capture her face. He
pulled her face to him, until her lips were only a breath
away from his. Quick, panicked, desperate breaths he
could count with her pulse.

''If I'm not Cameron Ross...''

Another breath. A sigh that incited sparks. "Yes?"

It was his turn to smile. "Then I'm not married to Cameron Ross's wife."

Even those tiny breaths stopped. Ethan knew, because his did, too. He heard insects chirruping. Birds screeching and trilling. The ocean, another world away, exhaling in surprise. And not a movement from Lilly.

"Does it..." she stopped. Sobbed, he thought, the sound swallowed so she didn't betray herself, even that close. "...make a difference?"

And Ethan, who had been so afraid, who had been so torn, who had been so guilty, laughed. He laughed, and he wrapped his hand around the back of Lilly's neck and pulled her that breath's space to meet him. And he kissed her.

He felt her shudder. He heard the catch in her breath. He tasted the surprise on her mouth. He closed his eyes, because he didn't need them after all, and he let Lilly know what kind of difference it made.

Tears. He tasted them on her cheeks. He sipped them like wine and kissed her eyes shut. Nectar. He tasted it on her tongue and shared it like forbidden secrets, sweet and dark and silken. Salt. Just a hint of it for spice, where it had collected along her throat, her throat that hummed at his touch. Slick and satiny and seductive.

"Oh, it matters," he groaned into her throat. "It matters a lot."

He didn't remember standing. He just knew he got there. He knew he walked Lilly back to that narrow, creaking iron bed. He eased her down onto it, so she was the one sitting and he the one kneeling. He just knew that his body, so sore and taut and tired, shivered like leaves in a high wind. He knew that his heart, which had felt so torn, thundered in exultation.

He just knew that finally, finally, he had Lilly in his arms, and he could finish all those half-finished wishes he'd been trying so hard to ignore.

He could feast himself on her warmth, sate his hands with her skin, soak his heart in her laughter. He wrapped his hands in her hair and pulled her mouth down to his. He devoured her with lips and teeth and tongue, and found her as hungry as he. Her hands, her skin, her bright, bubbling laughter that washed him like a mountain stream. He swept his own hands over her throat, and pulled the *mu'umu'u* easily over her shoulders. He let his mouth follow, stoking himself on the shivers on her sun-warmed skin. He followed it to the point where he could trace the swell of her breasts, dropping kisses along her collarbone to the hollow of her throat. He wrapped his arms around her and laid his head against her breasts, those sweet nourishing breasts he'd dreamed of. Full and proud and heavy in his hands, her nipples already taut. The color of pennies, he knew, even without opening his eyes, without pulling that sun-softened cotton lower. Blind, hungry, he closed his mouth over one of those nipples, took it with his teeth, suckled until the material was moist and Lilly was moaning, her head back, her hands in his hair, her body beginning to rock in age-old recognition.

"I knew," he whispered against her skin. "I knew...."

He took the other breast through the cotton, teasing his tongue with the textures. And he let his hands seek her waist, her hips, the strong, long lines of her legs, opening at his touch, inviting in silence the attentions he'd dreamed of, it seemed, forever.

Oh, she was like silk. Like sunlight and daydreams and promises of home. He felt her hands on him now, pulling his shirt free, burrowing and searching and inciting his own body to madness. She was killing him with those strong, silken hands. She was going to save him.

He discovered her beneath that plain, sacklike dress, there in the dark, his fingers finding her as impatient as he.

"Have you been dreaming of this, too?" he asked.

She laughed, shuddered. "I've been obsessing."

He smiled and pulled the *mu'umu'u* away. His pants followed, and that narrow cot held them both.

"Oh, you..." She couldn't seem to finish.

Considering what she was doing with her hands, Ethan couldn't so much as think. *There,* he wanted to scream. *There. No. No, not yet, I need to feel you around me. I need to...wait....*

So hot, so wet, so ready, and he had nothing left to compare this to. He didn't care. He had Lilly. He had now. He had a furious, blinding need to be inside her, to feel her seize around him and cry out. He needed to bury himself in her and never find his way free.

"Lilly..."

"Oh...shut up and...and..."

Her fingernails raking his back. Her voice a feline growl of desperation, her head rocking from side to side so that she spilled her hair over the pillow.

"Pennies," Ethan groaned against her. "I knew it. I knew...."

There was no material between them now. He reclaimed her breast, that taut, copper nipple a torment against his tongue, and he lifted himself, wanting to ask. To wait. She wrapped her hands around his buttocks and insisted. He was only human. He was sweating with the effort to hold on, to deny himself release until she had a chance.

"Ethan...*please*..."

She was bucking against him, scrabbling as if falling off a cliff, panting. Slick, so slick against his fingers, so ready, so perfect. He felt the first contractions, heard her gasp of astonishment, felt her head go back.

"E...*than!*"

Smiling, he slid into her.

And damn near came apart like a three-stage rocket.

He groaned; melting, shattering, swelling. Wrapping around her, losing control, losing everything as he felt her legs wrap around his waist, as he felt her body rock against his, pulling, pulling, as if she could devour him, too. He couldn't stop, couldn't wait, couldn't survive. He buried his head against her throat and let her welcome him. He buried himself in her, so far in her, so far into the hot, sweet depths of her that he knew he would never find his way back out. He closed his eyes, closed his ears, closed every sense he had except the shattering waves of heat and light and sound that swept him as he slammed into her and she screamed, laughing as she shattered around him, as she shattered him into a thousand pieces, shards of glass that reflected the sun, that lacerated him into senseless agony that could only be eased by crying out her name, again and again.

"Oh...oh..." She sobbed, laughed, held on as they fell into collapse on that narrow, creaky bed. "Oh, Ethan, I wish..."

Ethan rolled so that she lay against his chest. He wrapped his arms around her, his leg around her, and he rested around her. "What do you wish?"

For a second he didn't think she was going to answer.

"Oh," she managed, a hand against his heart, "that we didn't have to leave here."

Ethan smiled against her hair. "Me too. Think it's possible?"

She rubbed a little, as if to ease their way. "Nah. Sooner or later somebody'd stumble over us. Besides, you're going to have to explain to your cousin how you lost his boat."

Ethan unconsciously held her tighter, as if that would keep the rest of the world away a little while longer. "Well, for now, at least, let's be selfish. After all, the news is all good, isn't it?"

"Except for that pesky problem with those three kidnapers."

"Well, yeah. Except for that."

She rubbed again, a little more slowly, and settled more closely against him. "In that case, what's to worry about?"

Noah had had a bad enough day without having to deal with Ellen. But there she was, having another full set of hysterics all over Dulcy's shoulder. And Dulcy looked like she'd been up longer than Noah.

"Ellen," he snapped, stepping into the waiting room of the Coast Guard station, where they'd taken refuge from the circling press. "Enough! Falling apart isn't going to get Ethan back any faster."

"You don't understand," the blond beauty sobbed yet again, her hold on Dulcy's hand probably cutting off the blood supply to her fingers.

Noah walked over and untangled their fingers. "My wife is almost nine months pregnant, and I won't have you upsetting her even more. Now, settle down, or I'll have you shipped to the hotel."

Ellen straightened to her full height, which almost put her nose-to-nose with Noah. "You wouldn't dare. What would the press think?"

"That I like my wife more than you, probably. I don't give a damn."

"Have they heard anything?" Dulcy asked, rubbing gently at her belly in a curiously calming motion.

Exhausted and disheartened, Noah sat down next to her. "No. We're on a new shift of personnel. They don't know any more, but at least this liaison officer is kinder."

"The ransom's been paid?" Ellen asked.

Noah just nodded. Dropped into a trash container and watched, just as planned. And watched. And watched. It wasn't until later that they'd found that the container had been over a sewer lid. The kidnapers had cut a hole in the floor of the trash bin and come and gone before anybody had thought to check.

Which left them back at square one. No Ethan, no *Hannah Girl*. No word.

"It'll be all right," Dulcy said again, her warm hand now in his cold one. "Ethan's a survivor, Noah. You know that. Besides, he always said he was an ocean man."

Noah did his best to smile. "Yeah. At least he's not stuck on some mountain. God, he'd hate that like hell."

"How can you?" Ellen demanded in a whisper, huge eyes thick with tears. "How can you just sit here?"

"What do you think Noah should do, Ellen?" Dulcy asked. "Tear his hair out? Run down the street hoping to find the kidnapers on his own?"

"I don't know. I don't know! But you have to do something! He can't just be out there alone. Not the way he is."

Noah's head came up. "The way he is?"

Ellen sobbed, shoved a fist against her mouth.

Dulcy went very still. "What are you talking about, Ellen?"

Ellen wouldn't look at them. "He was putting it off until he'd made this trip for you. He knew how much you depended on getting away for roundup. But the minute he got home, he was going in. And now...now..."

Noah was on his feet. "Going in where?"

He'd thought he couldn't feel worse. He'd been wrong. He knew it the minute Ellen turned those liquid eyes at him and sobbed out the truth.

"Oh, God, he didn't want you to know. And you know how he is. He was just going to call you after."

Now Dulcy was on her feet. "After what?"

Ellen sobbed, and Noah wanted to strangle her.

"He was going to check into the hospital for experimental surgery. Noah, Ethan is going blind."

Ten

"Ethan."

"Mm-hmm."

"We need to call for help."

Lilly could tell Ethan was smiling. "I think we did jus[t] fine all by ourselves."

She laughed and blushed at the same time. "Fin[e] doesn't begin to cover it," she protested. Her body stil[l] glowed. Heck, her toes still tingled. She felt so alive So…powerful. She felt as if this were the most perfec[t] moment she was ever going to have.

Which it probably was.

Lilly didn't have any illusions. Ethan might not be [a] movie star, but he was still not hers. Not really. He be[-] longed to that outside world, with its mass communicatio[n] and migratory living patterns and power brokers.

A businessman. It sounded innocuous enough. But afte[r] knowing Ethan only a matter of days, she could say wit[h] all honesty that there wasn't anything innocuous about Ethan. Even injured. Even half-blind and dazed. He had his own *mana,* and Lilly had the feeling that once he rediscovered it, he would realize that hers wasn't strong enough to keep him. Not in that way, anyway. Her *mana* was meant for the mountains. Lilly of the earth. Caring Lilly. Not strong, beautiful, worldly Lilly, who could complement a successful businessman's life. Not charismatic, charming Lilly, who could keep him enthralled when he went back to those high-powered meetings and prestigious friends.

All she would get was this moment on this mountain, isolated from fear and futility and the famine of loneliness. And then she would carry it with her like a talisman to color the rest of her days.

Ethan began fingering her hair, and Lilly wanted to cry all over again.

"I think I've always liked blondes best," he murmured in a bemused voice.

Lilly couldn't even manage a good rise of indignation. "Most men do."

She was naked. Lying on her own mountain naked with the most singularly beautiful man she'd ever laid eyes on, ever been blessed enough to touch and love. She could warm the rest of her days just on the sound of his cries as he'd shuddered into her. Her name. Her simple, plain name, pulled from him like a revelation, and she'd done it. She'd made him swear and sweat and sing, and she would always have that to keep with her.

"I think I've just changed my mind," he murmured, wrapping himself just a little more tightly against her. "I think I've developed a decided fondness for brunettes."

No tears, she commanded herself, even as her body began to thrum with anticipation just from the touch of his naked skin. The jut of his pelvis, the pressure of his solid thigh, the hair-roughened planes of his belly and chest. His arms. Lilly could sing odes to his arms and symphonies to his hands. She could compose epic poetry about the smiles in those soft blue eyes, even knowing that when he'd held her, he'd closed them.

It didn't matter with Ethan. Lilly didn't care if he didn't see her.

"You just can't remember any blondes right now," she protested, focusing on the splay of her fingers against his chest. She wanted to go wandering again, follow bone and sinew like an explorer crossing a continent. She wanted to sate herself on the smell and sound and sight of him there in her arms on her mountain. But she was afraid to ask for more, afraid he would know how badly she needed it. Afraid, as always seemed to happen to her, that he would turn away.

So she held perfectly still, hardly breathing, listening to the song her body had begun to sing in praise of his proximity, and she tried to let that be enough.

"Lilly?"

"Mm-hmm?"

"Do you believe me when I say I never remember it being this good?"

Because she heard the humor in his voice, she laughed right back and smacked him. "You don't remember if you've had 'it' at all. But hey, I'll take any little compliment I can get."

Oddly enough, that impelled him to movement. He turned so that he was leaning over her a little, and he was frowning. "Stop it," he commanded, pushing her hair back from her face.

"Stop what?"

"Stop calling me a liar."

He seemed to lose interest in her hair. He was stroking her cheek, her throat, her shoulder, his concentration on her face, his smile soft and promising. Lilly couldn't breathe again. She could feel perfectly well that he wasn't lying. His body spoke eloquently of his satisfaction. His own renewed anticipation. And her body, completely without her permission, was answering. He was touching no more than her shoulder, his fingers light as the breeze, his smile soft as the rain, and she was melting, freezing, flying, right there on Uncle Danny's old army cot.

"Want me to prove it?" Ethan was asking in a voice that should have come with a warning.

Lilly felt like a deer in the headlights. "Prove what?" she asked, her voice high and breathy.

"That I'm not lying."

"Has it occurred to you that you're injured? We're gonna have some hiking to do pretty soon, ya know. You know how much you liked...oh...that..."

She couldn't keep her eyes open. She couldn't keep her toes from curling.

Ethan bent to lick her breast, and Lilly shattered into sunlight.

"I think I'm better now," he whispered against her damp skin, and she lost her objections.

She couldn't keep still. Her fingers seemed to search of their own will. Her body wrapped around his, seeking the sensation of his skin, his warm, rough skin and hard edges, his wise, smiling eyes and clever hands. She had hungered before. Now she memorized.

His shoulders, broad enough to block the sun, taut, hard shoulders for lifting, for holding, for protecting. His chest, wide and whorled with the kind of hair that tickled. His belly, so flat and sculpted, trembling beneath her touch. His legs, powerful, lean, a sculptor's imagination. She

captured them all with her hands, committing them to
memory like the tenets of a faith. She cupped his jaw in
her hands and winnowed her fingers through his thick,
rich hair. She kissed his eyes, those sweet, seductive eyes,
and she dipped her tongue into that tantalizing little cleft
at the edge of his chin.

And then…and then she returned to the myriad seduc-
tions of his mouth. She opened to him, she challenged
him, meeting him, exploring him, teeth and tongue and
lips, the textures slick and soft and dark. Hot, so hot. So
sinful she wanted to weep with it.

Her own body sang. It shivered, it soared, his hands
the wings of her flight. His fingers finding magic in the
nooks and crannies and secret places no one ever had
thought to seek. His mouth praising, pleading, searing her
with whisper and pleasure and honor. That body she had
so sought, those hands she'd watched, that face she'd
fought so hard to ignore, brought her light, brought her
wonder and wicked abandon. That injured, battered body
that shouldn't have been able to stand, created whirlwinds
in her that could only be quenched with his touch.

Lilly whimpered, she moaned, she rocked in his hands.
She pulled and coerced and commanded. And with a
smile, a smile that was only hers, Ethan came to her.

"Oh, Lilly," he moaned, voice ragged as old glass,
hands shaking and sweat-slicked, his face against her
throat. "I can't…can't wait.…"

Lilly laughed, her hands on his buttocks, her legs wrapping around him to urge him home. Closer, deeper, so full
in her she would explode, she would die, she would sweep
up beyond the mountains, the clouds, the sun itself, in his
arms.

"Come to me," she whispered into his ear, her body
knowing, her body readying, the sweet ache of wanting

him spinning through her, collecting in her like sunlight, deepening, brightening, tightening into lightning. Into thunder and windstorm. "Oh, Ethan...now..."

He pulled back, almost away, until she cried out in frustration, her body screaming with need for him, her mind a whirl of color and sound and sweet, whimsical music. He wrapped his hands in her hair, forced her to look at him, at those eyes that couldn't quite see her but saw her even better, at that smile that eclipsed the summer sun, at the glisten of sweat on his skin that betrayed his fight for control. He made her look at him, and then, with a sure stroke, he plunged into her. Deep, so deep, she had to gasp. So full she had to hold on, so right she had to cry out, her own body howling with the wonder of him, splintering into shards of light, convulsing around him as he met her, folded into her, rode with her, mounting the age-old rhythm of wonder and spinning out into space. Spilling, finally, hot and sweet and sighing, into her, where she wanted so much to keep him, there where no one else could have him, could take him away or talk him out of the beauty of that one, terrible moment of joining.

And then, slick and hot and spent, Lilly let him wrap her back into his arms and rest.

"Ethan."

"Mm-hmm."

"We *really* have to call for help now."

His fingers never stopped the languid stroking of her arm. "Why?" he asked, his voice matching the movement. "Did I break something?"

Lilly almost cried out. He'd meant it as a joke, of course. He couldn't have any idea how close his question had struck home. Yes, she thought, he'd broken something. He'd broken down every one of her barriers. Every

screen built of pragmatism and disappointment and fear
He'd hurt her far more than her Tutu Mary ever could
have done by claiming magic for her she'd never thought
to own. He'd proved she did. He'd shown her how, in his
hands, he could create in her the most powerful magic the
world had known. He could make her into a truly beautiful woman. A desirable woman with the power to make
a grown man weep.

And then, when he left, he would break her again. Because Lilly knew that when Ethan left this sacred mountain, he would take the magic with him. Lilly Malama
Kokoa, child of the earth, the practical child of practical
parents, had tasted bliss in the arms of this impossible
man. And she would never get to sample it again, because
when he left, as she knew he would, she would be forced
to walk off this mountain with her head high and her heart
hard, and she would have to return to the Lilly who had
sailed off this island just a few days ago. And only Lilly
would know what she'd lost.

Because now she wasn't sure whether she would ever
be able to climb these trails again after all.

But she wasn't the kind of person to hurt Ethan simply
because he didn't realize he was about to shatter her.

"We may be enjoying ourselves," she said, watching
her fingers again splayed across the slow murmur of his
heart, "but I doubt the kidnapers have simply given us a
time-out for sex."

"That wasn't sex," he disagreed, dropping a kiss into
her hair. "That was the earth moving. Or didn't you feel
it? For a minute I thought old Pele had woken up on this
island, too, and we were going to be showered with rocks
and lava."

It was amazing, Lilly thought. You could smile with a

knife in your chest. "*I* felt lava. But I still don't think Huey, Duey and Louise are going to care."

"I think Huey and Duey, at least, are gonna be jealous as hell."

Laughing, Lilly gave him a smack. "Come on, big important businessman. Let's finish fixing that radio, so you can let your cousin know you're all right."

That was the first thing she had said that got a reaction out of him. In fact, he bolted straight up, damn near rolling Lilly right off the bed.

"Oh, my God," he said. "Noah. You're right."

Lilly planted her bare feet on the floor to keep from landing on her nose and turned to where Ethan was reaching for his pants. "Noah?"

"My cousin."

She saw him wince when he moved and thought she should feel terrible. She didn't. Not about that, anyway. "You have another cousin?"

Ethan stopped, the ragged shorts all but zipped. "No..." His brow furrowed, and he closed his eyes. "Noah *is* Cameron. That's the secret. Part of the secret, anyway."

Lilly reached out to lay a hand on his arm. "That stage name we talked about?"

Ethan opened his eyes again, and Lilly saw the fragile light. "Exactly. Noah and Ethan, almost interchangeable. And Cameron Ross, whom we both created."

"Uh huh."

"But that's it. We sometimes...uh, pretend to be each other. To give Noah time away from celebrity. That's what I was doing on the boat."

Lilly should have felt better. "You remember?"

But he shook his head, which seemed to Lilly like the phone call from the governor staying execution just a little while longer. "No. Just leaving that day. Noah wanted to do roundup, and so I...uh, I took the *Hannah Girl* out to decoy the press. I told him I was going to spend a week in the islands and leave the boat there. But I had to get back.... I had..."

Lilly held on tighter. Ethan had that look, that almost frantic frown of frustration that made her hurt even worse than he.

"It's all right," she assured him, her mantra for his return to health. "You'll remember the minute you see him, Ethan. I promise."

But he was shaking his head. "I have to get back. I have to go to Philadelphia. It's vital."

She kept holding on, kept smiling. Kept wondering how much more she could take. "Then let's get going."

She set him up at the radio, but before she helped him, she helped herself to a bath in the mountain pool she loved so much. Surrounded by ferns and jasmine and hyacinth, scented with the tang of ginger and the soft, dark musk of decaying forest floor. Whispered to by water and old ghosts. The place where she belonged. The place she could no longer love, because the ghosts were all now displaced by Ethan's haunting laughter, the flowers dimmed before the sky of his eyes. The nurturing water and earth waning with the power of his arms.

Lilly wanted to stay there in the water searching for some comfort, but she knew she couldn't. So, slipping back into her *mu'umu'u* and tying back her hair, she walked back into the cabin in time to hear the static burst from the radio.

"We seem to have contact, Lilly." Ethan greeted her with a huge smile.

It was the hardest thing she'd ever done, but she smiled

right back. "In that case, move over. I just happen to have the code book."

She played with the radio, just like Uncle Danny had taught her, seeking the frequency that would do her the most good. Calling out into the world that waited beyond the walls of her mountain.

"Lilly? Lilly Kokoa, that you, girl?" an astounded voice answered her calls.

Lilly couldn't help but grin. "Sheriff Tanaka? How you doin'?"

"Question is, how *you* doin', girl? Where you at, hey?"

"Uncle Danny's cabin. Why? Dey lookin' me foah shuah?"

"You know bits of you boat show up you Tutu Mary's place? You mama, she be pullin' her hair, yeah?"

Lilly flushed. She'd forgotten. Caught up in her adventure, wrapped in the allure of a forbidden man who, at least for now, found her attractive, she'd just put her family away like old toys that had lost their attraction.

"You call her, Sheriff. Tell her I'm fine, hear? I need help gettin' down, do. You come?"

"You hurt, girl?"

"No. No, not me. Found somebody, heah? Some stupid boar hunter, get himself lost. He's *ho'okahi haole kane 'i'no*. You know de kine? Needs help *wikiwiki*."

There was a pause, more static. Lilly, knowing perfectly well that other people could hear, prayed that her uncle Danny's best friend didn't ask questions.

"You stay put, you hear? You uncle here harassin' me. We dere soon as can. Yeah?"

Lilly sighed with relief. "Yeah. Have Uncle Danny call home, yeah?"

"See you, Lilly Malama. Stay put."

And so Lilly signed off, knowing she should be glad.

Knowing, all the same, that her brief moment of magic was almost over.

"What did you say about me?" Ethan asked with a sly grin.

Lilly's answering smile was a little less assured. "Well, I figured our friends aren't fluent in Hawaiian, and I wanted Sheriff Tanaka prepared for trouble."

"A good idea. As long as he doesn't shoot me instead of the bad guys. What did you say?"

"That you were one bad *haole.* He'll bring help along." Finally, she grinned. "Sheriff Tanaka's one of my godfathers."

Ethan scowled. "I'll just hide under the floorboards 'til you give me the all-clear. How long 'til they get here?"

Not looking away from the radio, Lilly shook her head. "An hour or so, maybe."

Ethan grabbed her hands and smiled. "Race you to the swimming hole."

Without so much as a blink of hesitation, Lilly followed.

Ethan couldn't believe he could still stand up. He couldn't believe he felt so damn good.

Well, he could. How could he not, after sharing the most incredible day of his life with the woman lying next to him on the grass? It was as if he'd saved himself up for this moment, all his need, all his desire, all his hunger, to be expended in her arms. Ethan looked down at her, lying alongside him, her hair her only ornament, her warmth his only protection. The sun was settling behind the next ridge, and the light was poured, like honey, over Lilly's skin. He could tell. He could see color, could damn near taste it on his tongue.

He cherished her. Her laughter, her sense, her calm,

quiet compassion. He'd known her a matter of days when he hadn't known anything else, but still, he thought he hadn't known anybody like her. He thought he might never again. He knew that somehow he had to return to her.

After he went home. After he did what he needed to do.

It still nagged at him, a burr under the saddle. He had to go back for something. Or someone. He just didn't know what or who or why, and it eroded his contentment like breakers at a limestone cliff.

But for now, this brief, perfect moment, he had Lilly. He had the old echoes of this place that seemed to welcome him more than anywhere else had, he thought. He had a perfect, unruffled peace.

But the cavalry was coming, and the last thing Lilly needed, when she seemed to know everybody on the island, was to be caught *in flagrante* with a stranger at her uncle Danny's cabin. So with one last kiss to that impossibly smooth brow, he got to his feet.

"Time to come in from play," he whispered to her.

She stretched like a cat, and Ethan thought again of their play in the water. Their slow lovemaking that had tumbled out onto the grass. The silent completion there among the flowers and the rustle of the wind.

"I'll be there in a minute," she said. "My *mu'umu'u*'s still here. That is, if it isn't all ripped."

Ethan combed her hair with his fingers. "You wouldn't come in and play. I had to help."

Lilly laughed, and Ethan fell further under her spell. "Y'know, if it weren't for that bullet hole I patched up and the condition of your face, I'd be tempted to say that that story about injuries sustained was just a sham to get

me to do most of the work walking up here. You sure
haven't shown any disabilities since.''

''You inspire me.''

''You exhaust me,'' she countered easily. ''And I'm
not wearing a shiner the size of a dinner plate.''

Ethan climbed to his feet and stretched. ''Trust me,
Lilly,'' he said, automatically flinching from the protest-
ing body parts. ''I'm not completely unaffected. I just
found the temptation impossible to overcome.''

He would also need a three-day nap to reclaim his energy. But then, he was about to get the chance for it,
wasn't he? And by the time he got over it, he would be
able to pull Lilly out of that house with all the brothers
and start over where he'd left off.

Bending very gingerly, he reclaimed his shorts and slid
them on. He'd been there a day and he'd lost the urge to
wear a shirt. Or shoes, for that matter. Or maybe he never
wore shoes, considering the condition he'd woken up in.
And then, because he knew he should give Lilly that all-
important propriety space, he limped down the hill toward
the cabin.

And squinted.

''Hey, Lil,'' he said, walking a little faster. ''Get your
stuff together. I think the cavalry's here already.''

He heard the sudden rustle of clothing behind him, but
his attention was caught. He needed to get farther away
from her. Especially if that was her uncle Danny who was
just stepping into the cabin.

Funny. Now that they were here, he wasn't sure he
wanted them to save him after all. He wanted to see Noah,
of course. He wanted to touch his cousin, just to make
sure he hadn't made him up out of a need for easy answers. But he didn't want to leave this magic place. That

magic woman. He didn't want the rest of the world intruding on his perfect moment of happiness.

Which was probably why he wasn't really attending when he opened the door. His mind was back at the pool with Lilly. He saw the fatigues, heard the snap of a voice that carried authority, and only wondered at the last moment what seemed wrong.

"Who are you?" he asked, seeing that the person in fatigues was a woman. "We were expecting the sheriff."

Did she smile? He didn't know. He just saw her straighten. "Coast Guard," she said. "It's a real relief to see you, Mr. Campbell. A lot of people have been looking for you."

Ethan smiled. "Is my cousin with you?"

"No, sir. Not yet. Is Ms. Kokoa with you?"

"Yeah. She's just up the hill. I'll get her."

"Uh, no, sir," the woman said. "You won't."

Ethan had been in the process of turning back out the door. Instead, he faced the woman one more time, and that was when he knew what was wrong.

"I recognize your voice," he said.

Now he knew she smiled. Probably because she had a gun in her hand. "That's right, Mr. Campbell. Now, why don't we all sit down?"

Ethan spun on his heel to warn Lilly. But he saw her just outside—caught tight in the arms of either Duey or Louise. With the other two following just behind.

All their work, all that effort.

"Why don't you sit down, Mr. Campbell?"

Mr. Campbell sat down.

Eleven

"**A**re you all right?" Ethan and Lilly asked each other simultaneously.

Both smiled, as if they weren't at gunpoint again.

"I'm sorry," Ethan apologized, sitting on the hard iron bed. "I seem to be nothing but bad luck for you, Lilly."

"Well, if she didn't have bad luck..." one of the hapless trio of kidnapers intoned on a curious giggle.

"Enough," the Coast Guard Lieutenant snapped. "We wasted too much time getting up here. We don't need to waste more on the Three Stooges."

"We told you it was steep," Louise complained.

"I thought you'd be able to find an easier way, being Hawaiian and all."

"How many times we gotta tell you?" Louise demanded. "We're not Hawaiian. We're Italian!"

"Italian, Hawaiian, who the hell cares? You're idiots. Now sit her down and shut up."

Lilly landed on the single chair with a thump and did her best to ignore the staccato of her heart. They'd come so close. God, she'd almost had a stroke when she'd heard that odd, throaty chuckle of Louise's out by the pool. And now this. She was sitting in her beloved cabin with a gun at her neck, and Ethan was hunched over on the bed, his hands tied behind his back. Even if the kidnapers hadn't hurt him again, he'd exerted himself quite enough on those broken ribs to be suffering for it now.

Just the thought of what kind of exertions Ethan had been involved in made Lilly flush. She didn't realize she'd giggled until everybody turned to her. Which made her flush again.

"Time to bring Ethan back to his relatives, huh?" she asked to throw them off.

The woman in the fatigues glared at her. "You can't be that stupid."

"I think optimistic would be a better term," Ethan corrected with a gentle smile.

Lilly saw the smile, saw the curiously intent expression in his eyes that didn't quite match it, and knew he was trying to communicate something. Considering the fact that the rescue party was due at any moment, and considering the fact that the kidnaping party wouldn't want anybody left around to greet them, Lilly didn't need ESP to know that Ethan was hoping she could help him stall a bit. She just wasn't sure how he also expected to overcome the uneven odds.

"You really are in the Coast Guard?" he was asking the new person. "I assume you're the boss."

The woman dipped her head a bit, like a queen accepting tribute. "That's why it's worked so well so far. I've been able to throw everybody off the scent while keeping track of their progress. The search grid should be here soon.''

Which meant she didn't know they'd made the call yet. Should Lilly feel better? Should she find a way to turn so she could look out the window for Uncle Danny and Sheriff Tanaka? She'd been happy to accept Ethan's unspoken belief that Huey, Duey and Louise were incompetent, but she couldn't say the same about this brisk, hard-eyed little woman. Since she hadn't introduced herself, Lilly figured she might as well follow the Huey, Duey and Louie theme and name her Daisy. Besides, Lilly thought, with another near-giggle, she walks like a duck.

"By the way," Daisy was saying to her. "The missing person report didn't quite go in on you yet."

Lilly just nodded. "Oh."

Please, Uncle Danny, she prayed. Be careful. Be careful for Ethan. He's in such peril right now. And I'm so useless in a situation like this.

A librarian against kidnapers. It was even more ludicrous than that movie Ethan's cousin had made. Even if she was only trying to figure out how to save a businessman instead of the president of the United States.

"I can assume you got the money already?" Ethan was asking, as if discussing the weather.

Even Huey, Duey and Louise snapped to attention.

"Three million," Daisy said with some satisfaction.

"Uneven split," Ethan mused distractedly. "It would have been better to get four million."

"I assume you can afford that?" Lilly asked him.

"Well, I think I can," he retorted, a glint of humor giving him away.

Lilly snorted unkindly. "I think you're just trying to inflate your worth."

Those high giggles of terror were crowding her throat

Her hands were clenched in her lap, and her chest was impossibly tight. She'd been afraid before, when she'd looked up from her little sailboat to see guns pointed at her. Now she was almost hysterical. The guns were pointed at Ethan. And she loved Ethan.

And Ethan, damn it, was laughing. "Leave it to me to get kidnaped with the only woman who fails to fall under my spell."

Lilly couldn't help it. "Remembering more, are you?"

"Excuse me," Daisy objected, waving her assault weapon a little, "I believe I'm the one in charge here."

"Now you know why we had such a hard time," Huey groused to no one in particular.

"You had a hard time because you're idiots," his boss snapped.

"Without us idiots," Duey said, "you wouldn't'a found this cabin. Would ya?"

Louise snickered. "Not bad for Italians."

"Can I ask a question?" Lilly asked.

"No!" the four answered.

She shrugged. "I was just wondering how come you couldn't talk one Hawaiian into doing the job. Not all of us are pure of heart, you know."

Daisy scowled. "I thought they *were* Hawaiians."

It sounded as if she were being strangled, but Lilly laughed. "How long have you been stationed out here, Lieutenant?"

"A month."

"Well, that explains it. I mean, we do all look alike."

"Let's get *on* with it!" Louise objected. "We do still have to kill 'em and get all the way back down the damn trail before sundown, ya know."

"Good point," Ethan said with a nod. "Although you could actually go the other way. You're closer."

"No boat over there," Huey said.

"And I ain't walking *up* another foot," Louise agreed.

Lilly nodded agreeably. "It is steep. Although I imagine the Italian Alps are just as steep, aren't they?"

"Beats me," Duey answered. "I was born in Jersey."

"If I was born in Jersey, I'd move to Hawaii, too," Ethan said, then grinned. "Hey, I think I remembered something else."

"Shut up or I'll shoot you now!" Daisy screeched.

"Aren't you going to shoot us anyway?" Lilly asked, giddy and sweaty and shaking.

"And leave evidence? Maybe you *are* stupid."

"They intend to make it look as if we made a wrong turn and slid off a cliff, so they won't get snagged for kidnaping *and* murder," Ethan informed her.

Lilly's stomach somersaulted. "Oh. Of course. Silly me."

Was now the moment to remind everyone that the penalties for kidnaping didn't go up with murder? The bane of a research librarian's memory. Too full of useless trivia, like the Lindbergh Law. Surely there was some other bit of trivia she had stored away that could help them? Distract the bad guys. Convince them that murder just wasn't a good option, no matter how well they'd seen all four of their faces.

Which was when she heard it. Over the sound of Duey's bad adenoids and Huey's scratching, and the constant rush of water from outside; a clear three-note whistle, and then a trill. Then, seconds later, repeated.

Wondering how much punishment her skittish stomach could take from sudden cycles of hope and despair, Lilly lifted her head. "Huh."

Everybody looked at her.

"'Huh'?" Daisy demanded. "What 'huh'?"

Lilly shook her head, still listening. Hoping they couldn't see the sudden tremble of her white-knuckled hands. "Oh, I'm sorry, nothing. I just didn't know they were still on Molokai."

Everybody looked around.

"They? They who?"

Lilly smiled as if it were the most delightful thing in the world. "The *'o'u*. Hear it? Three-note trill and then a whistle. It's a forest songbird. I thought they were only on the Big Island and Kauai anymore. This is such a treat."

It was her turn to pass messages just with her eyes. And she knew Ethan couldn't see her. Maybe he could hear it in her voice.

"You're about ten minutes from biting the big one, and you're worrying about *birds?*" Louise demanded.

Lilly shrugged. "I like birds. I especially like to find birds where you don't expect them, you know?"

"I know exactly," Ethan enthused. "Why, once I saw a ruby-throated warbler in my front yard."

"You like birds, too?" Lilly asked.

Ethan's smile would have done a pirate proud. "Love 'em. I'd sure love to see that *'o'u.*"

"I can arrange that," Daisy snapped. "Midair, as you're cartwheeling off the cliff."

Ethan frowned. "Oh, I wish that wasn't what you had in mind. I'm afraid of heights."

She giggled like a schoolgirl. "Well, don't look down." And then she pulled him to his feet. "Time to go, kids. We don't have all day, ya know. Some of us have a bit of advantageous disappearing to do."

His hands tied behind his back, Ethan wobbled a little before finding his balance. "On the *Hannah Girl,* I presume."

The boss smiled. "Actually, it's now the *Capital Gains*. Cute, huh?"

"Delightful."

Lilly found herself on her feet and turned toward the door. "I don't suppose we can rethink this plan?"

Louise gave her an unfriendly shove. "Out."

Lilly flexed her hands. She took a surreptitious breath to calm herself. She heard the birdcall a third time from a completely different direction and knew that the cavalry was all there, and all in place. She just had to make sure she and Ethan stayed out of the line of fire.

And Ethan was in the process of walking out the cabin door.

Lilly didn't really have to fake the panic in her voice. "Oh, God!" she all but wailed. "I don't want to die!"

Louise gave her a shove that should have sent her through the wall. Lilly made sure it sent her through Daisy, who was guiding Ethan down the step into the yard. Lilly, Daisy and Ethan all tumbled to the ground.

"What the—"

Daisy was trying to raise her gun. Lilly reached for it. She heard the thunder of feet from around the back of the cabin and felt the hard kick Louise delivered to get her back up. She also felt Ethan struggling to right himself like a tipped beetle.

"Stay down," she panted, hands around Daisy's so she could pull that gun away, knee in Daisy's back.

"I t'ink you wanna put dat down," a basso voice announced with great amusement somewhere behind her.

Louise screeched. Duey whined. Huey evidently remembered his training, because even with at least four heavily armed men charging down on them, he managed to get a gun tucked nicely into Lilly's ear just about the moment Daisy got one shoved untidily into Ethan's chest

Everybody stopped.

Lilly was facedown, inches away from Ethan. She could smell the earth, she could hear the chatter of water and the rasp of heavy breathing. Probably those damn adenoids again. But mostly she saw Ethan, just as facedown as she, just as caught. Ashen-faced and sweating and silent. But smiling. Smiling at her as if this were all a wicked joke that only the two of them shared.

And, unbelievably, he got her to smile, too.

"You okay, Lilly Malama?" her uncle Danny asked in a deceptively nonchalant voice.

"Fine, foah shuah," she answered, even with the sweat trickling into her eyes and her heart rate setting new land-speed records. "But, you know, Ethan been bettah."

"I think we have a Mexican standoff here," Daisy said from where she was resting most of her weight on Ethan's back.

"Maybe," Sheriff Tanaka said. "But how you gonna get off dis hill we no let you go?"

"You're going to escort us. We get away, we let these two live."

"What if we don't want 'em back?" Uncle Danny asked.

"Then we'll be more than happy to leave you all up here...in whatever condition we see fit."

This was met by a round of masculine laughter. "I t'ink maybe you got dat all the way 'round, yeah?"

"I think maybe you want to get Cameron Ross's cousin back to him."

Now Lilly heard a couple of whistles of astonishment. She saw Ethan still smiling, still panting with discomfort from Daisy's knee in his back. She smelled her own terror, sour and pungent, and she knew they couldn't stay that way. She also knew, even before he did anything, that Ethan was about to try to save her.

So she moved first. "I'll lead you down the hill," she said. "I'll go with you until you can get away, if you want. Two of these men are my uncles, and another is my cousin, so they won't hurt you if you have me. Besides, Ethan isn't going to make it back down the mountain. You can see how bad he is."

"Lilly—" three separate voices warned at once, one of them Ethan's.

"Oh, come on," she insisted. "I'm lying here with a gun in my ear, and it isn't going to move until somebody makes a decision. And, Uncle Danny? I don't like having a gun in my ear."

"Foah shuah, girl."

"They need a Hawaiian to show them the shortcut down," she insisted.

And since her uncles were Hawaiian, she didn't need to say that her uncles would know an even shorter cut.

"Lilly, don't," Ethan pleaded.

Lilly looked away.

He didn't understand. This was her home court, these were her friends. And he was her love. She couldn't let anything happen to them, and she knew better than he how to prevent it, here, at least, on her own mountain.

In the end, Lilly walked back down the mountain with Huey, Duey, Louise and Daisy. They didn't tie her hands because she needed them for balance. They didn't question her when she took trails they hadn't, because they knew she really was a Hawaiian. And when she walked them through the hottest, wettest, steepest part of the rain forest, they slogged along behind, secure in the knowledge that they'd left all her relatives and their famous hostage tied up at that little cabin near the ridge.

So it was that Lilly was the only one not surprised when two hours later, after walking her exhausted captors into heatstroke, the forest trail suddenly came alive with shrieks and whistles and large, flying bodies. Lilly dropped and rolled like a burn victim until she was clear of the fire zone, and lay there, arms tucked over head, heart hammering, until the gunfire stopped and her uncle laughed.

"You one powerful *wahine*," he praised her. "You *tutu*, she be proud as peacock."

Gingerly, Lilly lifted her head to see each of the kidnapers topped by a burly, black-haired man, all of them grinning like kids. Then and only then did she launch herself to her feet and fly into her uncle Danny's arms.

"I knew you'd take care of things!" she laughed, hugging and kissing the huge man until he blushed scarlet. And then she repeated the treatment for each of the men, even Sheriff Tanaka, who was calling for some kind of backup on his walkie-talkie.

"I knew if you wore 'em out enough, we wouldn't have any trouble," he said. "Your man said you worth ten police, yeah?"

"My—" Lilly stopped, instinctively looked uphill. "Is he all right? Did you leave him in the cabin?"

"Why, no, we..."

Everybody was looking around now.

"Uh oh," Uncle Danny muttered.

"He came down with you?" Lilly demanded, outraged. "You made him walk this trail?"

"No way we could keep him away, little Lilly. That boy *pupule nui* foah you, yeah? He don't take no for an answer. Anybody see Lilly's *haole?*"

"Ethan!" Lilly was yelling, frantically pushing through foliage that could have hidden an elephant.

"He knocked me over," Huey offered from where he was sitting on the ground, his hands tied behind his back. "Otherwise I coulda put one in your big, Hawaiian butt."

Lilly ran that way. So did everybody else. But it was Lilly who tripped over bare feet. It was Lilly who realized they belonged to Ethan and dropped to his side. It was Lilly who saw all the fresh blood. It was Lilly who realized that Ethan had finally tripped over something that would probably kill him.

"Uncle Danny!" she wailed, Ethan already in her arms. "Oh, God, Uncle Danny!"

Uncle Danny came. Sheriff Tanaka called for backup again, and Uncle Mike lifted Ethan like a child and carried him at a run the rest of the way to the bottom of the cliff, where a helicopter could lift him off the beach in a rescue basket.

It was Cousin Kumu who stayed behind to see to the kidnapers with the sheriff. It was Uncle Pono who rowed Lilly out to the *Hannah Girl* and turned that powerful sleek cabin cruiser towards Oahu, where Ethan had been taken and the kidnapers would follow. And it was also Uncle Pono who walked like a silent warrior alongside his queen when Lilly strode into the trauma center to demand information on Ethan's condition. It was Pono she turned to when she found out the truth.

The nurse took one look at Lilly's dirty, tattered appearance and set down what she was doing. "Come with me," she said with a soft, sad smile. "Somebody wants to see you."

She led Lilly past the public areas to a quiet, carpeted corridor that seemed to whisper of tension and pain. Lilly could almost feel the flutter of injured hearts in this place. She could hear the stridor of stressed and failing lungs. She couldn't bear it. Couldn't breathe. She couldn't stay in this sterile, hard place where sickness was battled like an army, instead of coerced to leave like a bad visitor.

She walked anyway, her small hand engulfed in Uncle Pono's, her heart shrinking from the things she knew with the magic her *tutu* had seen. Head high, she faced the thing she feared the most, because she knew that Ethan was suffering here.

When the nurse opened a door into the small waiting room, Lilly caught her breath. For just a moment she thought that Ethan stood before her. Whole, healthy, handsome.

But it was another Ethan. A weary, frightened Ethan with lines of pain on his face that had nothing to do with physical discomfort. An Ethan who usually had more charisma, more presence. Who now looked like nothing more than a grieving brother.

"You're Noah," Lilly breathed before she thought of it.

And she let go of Pono's hand to take both of his.

For an eternity, he said nothing. Just held on to her hands as if he could borrow something from her. Which he did. Lilly offered him her strength, her healing, her wisdom. Her love. For this was the man who was the shadow of her Ethan, and Ethan loved him enough to suborn his own needs and wants for him.

His eyes widened for a moment, as if he could actually name the force that passed between them. His lips curled into a hesitant smile.

"I know a little of what you did for Ethan," he said, his voice gravelly and sore. "But I'm afraid I—"

"Lilly," she said with a smile. "My name is Lilly Kokoa. Please tell me how he is."

She knew as surely as she knew her own island that this man knew everything she felt for his cousin. He gave her hand a squeeze but refused to let go. "He's in surgery," he said. "They're...uh, hopeful."

Lilly wasn't sure whether it was his pain or hers that twisted her heart. Maybe both. It was certainly strong enough to drop her. She felt her uncle Pono stand close beside her, because, of course, he knew.

"Would you like to sit with us?" Noah asked. "Tell us everything that happened?"

Lilly sucked in a calming breath. "Thank you."

She saw Dulcy then. Lilly knew her as if she'd met her out there on those mountains of hers. Tiny, redheaded, great with child. A spark of such sweet strength in those sharp gray eyes.

Lilly found herself laughing. "I hope you aren't expecting that little boy to wait 'til you get back to Montana."

If Lilly had known how much, with her wild black hair and calf-length dress and wise eyes, she resembled her *tutu*, whose *mana* was legend, she would have been surprised. But the tiny woman who greeted her wasn't so much surprised by her appearance as comforted.

"He's already made that eminently clear to me," she said with a soft smile. "Sit down, Lilly. I'm—"

Lilly nodded. "Dulcy. I know. It's wonderful to meet you." More wonderful than Dulcy would ever know, Lilly thought with a silly smile. "This is my uncle Pono, who helped us today."

Introductions were made and, bit by bit, the story told. And when, finally, Lilly finished with the hard truth that Ethan had been injured this last time trying to pull her out of a fire she'd set herself, it was Dulcy who reached across and held her hand. "Ethan's the biggest klutz in the contiguous forty-eight states. Don't blame yourself because out of all that gunfire he caught a bullet or two."

Lilly blanched all over again. "Two?"

"Dose fast guns, Lilly Malama," Pono said softly beside her.

Lilly felt again the exquisite pain of picking Ethan up off that forest floor.

"Something else," she said, not wanting to give these people any more pain. Knowing she must. "I know he was trying to hide it from me, but his eyes...something was wrong with his eyes."

Another flash of grief in those legendary sky-blue eyes, a quick grasp of his hand by his tiny wife. A soft, sad smile. "We know. We found out that he put off an operation he needed on his eyes to help me out."

"An operation?"

He shrugged. "I don't know the details. It's experimental, is all I've heard. Without it..."

Without it, Lilly would always be beautiful, at least in Ethan's eyes. Even so, Lilly rejoiced. At least, she thought, she knew where he'd needed to go. She knew that he would regain what had meant so much to him.

"He also hasn't remembered everything," she said. "Even hearing who you were, I'm not sure—"

Noah reached across and took her hand with his free one. Lilly could feel the strength, the purpose, of those two people and knew why Ethan could easily give up so much for them. "That's not something to worry about. We'll have all the time in the world to get him back."

He gave her another squeeze for emphasis, and Lilly smiled. For them. For herself.

"Mr. Ross?" a new voice intruded.

Everybody stood up to greet a grimy, rumpled woman in surgical scrubs. Everybody held their breath until she pulled off her cap, scratched her graying hair and smiled.

"He's a tough son-of-a-bitch," she admitted. "Which,

considering all the injuries he seems to have suffered recently, is what has kept him going.''

"But—"

She waved a hand. ''You can pay me an exorbitant fee, but most of the good work was already done. Amazing what those old herbs can manage when used right. I just took out the bullets. Oh, and his spleen and a small piece of his liver. But if he keeps doing as well as he has, he'll be fine.''

Lilly almost landed in a heap on the floor. Noah cried out and caught his wife in his arms. Uncle Pono leaned over and whispered in Lilly's ear.

And Lilly, after a few more moments of assuring herself that everything was all right, promising she would be back to check on things, left with her uncle to let her parents know that she was safe.

And it was on the way out, as she passed that same first nurse, that Lilly lost the joy she'd just reclaimed. There was a woman standing at the desk whom Lilly almost felt she should have known. Tall, sleek, blond, dressed like a businesswoman and commanding attention like a lawyer at trial.

"You will show me back to where Cameron Ross is waiting,'' she insisted to the nurse, who didn't seem all that impressed. "He's waiting for word on Ethan Campbell.''

"We can only let relations back, ma'am,'' the nurse was saying.

The woman straightened even farther, huge tears appearing in her blue eyes. "Relation?'' she shrilled. "I'm Ethan Campbell's wife!''

Lilly didn't even feel Uncle Pono's hand on her arm. She just let him walk her out the door and back into the life she should never have left in the first place.

Twelve

Lilly did everything she could to prove to her family that she was all right. She went back to work, she baby-sat her sister's two toddlers, she signed up for post-grad courses in Hawaiian culture at U of H. She smiled and laughed and hugged, and she relied on her extensive network of family and friends to hide her from the press when they found out that she'd been instrumental in saving Cameron Ross's beloved cousin.

While doing her best to downplay her part in the adventure, she surreptitiously followed Ethan's progress. It was easy to do, since the press was chock-full of his battle for life. From critical to stable to discharged, with a few pictures and the inevitable bedside confessions of his distraught cousin. Then off to Philadelphia, flown by Cameron Ross himself, to get his near-identical sky-blue eyes treated. Early on, she'd even sneaked into the hospital, always in the dead of night when only the unearthly green of monitor lights lit Ethan's face. She'd taken his hands, just as her *tutu* had taught her, and she'd poured every ounce of strength she had into him. And then, before anybody could find out, she'd slipped away.

Never a word was said about the amnesia, although the blond wife made it into more than one photo op. Lilly kept one of the pictures in her room, taunting herself with the difference in their looks. Proving to herself with one grainy photo how inappropriate it was to have thought that Ethan Campbell, with memory intact, would choose to waste his time on plain little Lilly Kokoa.

And, as if she hadn't had the message shoved home with that, Lilly had to suffer through the notoriety she'd suddenly gained. She made it through the first round of Exotic-Dancer-Saves-Famous-Cousin headlines and stiffly ignored the camera lenses in the audience at the afternoon show. She even acquiesced when her boss, finding her notoriety to be oddly bad for business—since it was tough to get paying customers past the reporters—asked her to take a short leave of absence until the furor died down. But it was when one of the morning talk-show hosts commented on the fact that of all the notorious beauties in the Hawaiian islands for Ethan Campbell to be rescued by, he'd had the bad luck to stumble over a woman who looked like she'd taken a whack in the face with a shovel, that she gave in to the inevitable and escaped to her Tutu Mary's on Kalaupapa.

"Where you *mana*, little Lilly?" her tutu asked with a frown.

She was in her seventies, this magnificent old woman with the diamond-bright eyes. Her face was ravaged, her hands clubs that would never sing the hula again, and her left foot a replacement. But Lilly, especially after spending her time on Tutu Mary's mountain, saw only the force.

The majesty and grace in a woman as old and young as the islands she so loved.

Lilly went to her like a child and told her everything. She told her what she'd never said to her mother, even though she knew her mother understood perfectly well. She told her Tutu Mary about the love she'd found, the magic she'd unearthed, the power she'd unleashed. She told her of the mistake she'd made. And after listening, her Tutu Mary just sighed and held her, like the child she wished she still were, and she sang the old songs and told the old stories, and Lilly at least was comforted.

Lilly spent two weeks with her Tutu Mary. She walked among the graves of her ancestors and pulled on her traditional dress to dance the hula there on the island where it had been born, her movements given to the water and the land and the sky alone. She grieved as if she'd lost a part of herself and she vowed to go on. She sat at her *tutu*'s knee and asked her how to use this pain to help her grow. She wept and she chanted and she thought, there in the most beautiful place on earth, a verdant slice of heaven at the edge of a mighty ocean, where only cemeteries and hospitals and sad, dignified ghosts survived. She spent an afternoon sitting in St. Philomena's Church, built by Father Damien for his lepers so long ago, and she remembered balance.

She straightened her back for the first time since she'd walked out of that trauma center, and she went back to Oahu to get on with her life. And only her Tutu Mary really knew how much of the spark had gone from her wide black eyes.

"When you gonna answer those phone calls, Lilly?" her mother asked one morning over breakfast.

Trying very hard to read a treatise on ancient land uses,

Lilly took a second to look up. "You'd think the press would have gotten tired of me by now. It's been a month."

But her mother, who had, indeed, combined the Portuguese and Hawaiian genes into a delicate, high-cheeked beauty that only seemed to mature as the gray crept into her lustrous black hair, frowned. "I'm not talking about those jackals. I'm talking about Mr. Ross. He called again. Didn't Jess tell you?"

Just as every other time she'd heard the news, Lilly felt her heart constrict. Instinctive fear that something was wrong with Ethan. That he needed her. Then, quickly, a dose of cold water, knowing that she was not the person to answer such a summons anymore. Even so, she had to ask.

"Is there a problem with Ethan?" she asked.

Her mother shook her head. "Not that he said. He just wanted you to call him back." For a second, she smiled. "He said he wanted you to know he was impressed with your safety net. It was the first time in about a decade that he hadn't had a phone call returned."

Lilly couldn't help smiling back. "It'll do his humility some good."

"He's a nice man, though, isn't he?"

Lilly nodded. "He's a very nice man. I guess I really should call him back. I want to know where to send a present for the baby."

The baby named Ethan McCann Campbell, who had been delivered while Lilly was on Kalaupapa. Lilly had known, standing out by the surf, the minute Dulcy had gone into labor. She'd known, deep in places she still didn't quite acknowledge, the moment Noah Campbell had first laid eyes on his new son. And standing out there, alone with the wind and waves, she'd known when the baby's new godfather had first held him in arms still hooked up to IVs and monitors there in the intensive-care unit.

"Call him soon," her mother said as she got to her feet. "It's not polite to ignore him."

And it wasn't healthy to pine after his cousin. Lilly gathered her papers back together and climbed to her feet in her tiny, ramshackle kitchen. Her mother was washing dishes at a sink strung in seashells, and the table sat beneath a window festooned in colored fishing net and starfish. The cheap, whimsical decorations of a family without money. A family who had survived in the canning factories and cane fields of an island that had once been theirs. A family who had never needed the things the rich *haoles* brought with them to the expensive resorts that ringed the island like beads on a broken necklace.

Lilly had never really looked at her house before. At her big, beautiful family. She looked now, with eyes reopened by her visit with Ethan's family. She remembered what was important, and she found herself glad for it. She realized that at least she could never be accused of wanting Ethan for any money he might have had. She wouldn't have known what to do with it.

Except, maybe, buy the valley of her ancestors.

She was going to call. She really was. But first she had another shift at the hotel. Another eight hours in front of tourists who sucked down mai tais and blue Hawaiians as she retold ancient stories.

Her application was in at the Polynesian Cultural Center. It wouldn't pay as much, but it wouldn't be as tough to get through, either. At least while she continued to investigate this rare gift her *tutu* had given her. This gift Ethan had given her permission to own.

Lilly Malama Kokoa had always been a practical child.

A practical woman. As she gathered her things together for work in the tiny bedroom she used to share with her sister, she knew that she would never love anybody else as she had Ethan Campbell. She would never look in anyone else's eyes and see herself so clearly again. Maybe someday she would find some nice man who would accept her, who would endure her passions and questions and mysteries, and offer companionship. Maybe she would have children. Maybe she wouldn't. She did know, though, that because Ethan Campbell had been in her life, she would never look at her world the same way again. Or at herself. And because of that, she would always be thankful she'd had him. Even for that brief, miraculous moment. Even knowing that she could never have him again.

She also knew that, for the first time in her life, the islands of her home weren't enough for her. Because, for the first time in her life, her family wasn't contained in them.

The hotel was a high-rise on the edge of the sea. Gleaming, expensive, manicured and modeled to fulfill every fantasy a *haole* could have of tropical delight. Beautiful women lay scattered on pool-deck chairs like bright flowers. Children screamed and splashed in the water. Waiters in vivid flowered shirts circled with trays heavy with pastel-colored drinks. The trade wind blew, and at the edge of the property the water washed up on Waikiki Beach. It was a perfect day in paradise.

"Ladies and gentlemen, this afternoon, we have the pleasure of presenting a little of Hawaii's special color. If you'll turn your attention to the upper deck, may we present the Hukilau Dancers."

A scattering of applause from those not too immersed

in their *People* magazines and mai tais. An abrupt cessation of the canned music on the sound system. And then, in a line like exquisite pearls, a dozen girls in grass skirts and leis and hibiscus flowers tucked in thick black hair sidled out from the hotel in an undulating line.

He sat back in his chair as if he were just another visitor, doing his best to control his pulse rate. Would he know her? Would he want to? He'd convinced Noah to let him come alone, even though he was still in dark sunglasses to counteract the tropical sun and easily tired from all the excavations that had been done on his poor body. Even though she hadn't returned one of Noah's calls, as if she never wanted to hear his name again.

He couldn't help it. He had to find out for himself.

He had to know that he hadn't imagined what had happened out on that mountain.

He sipped at his mai tai and held his breath and tried to remember what she'd said. Third from the left? Third from the right?

Not the third on the left. Not enough hair. The third from the right was too tall.

He thought.

He was sweating, and he hadn't even talked to her yet. So he began from the end.

A beautiful girl, all eyes and bright white teeth. Slim, swaying body that should have sent any red-blooded man into a swoon.

But not his Lilly Malama. She didn't move correctly.

The same for the next, and the next after. Beauties such as only these islands seemed to breed—liquid eyes and skin the color of honey and lush, limber figures.

Again for the fourth. The fifth.

Lilly, where are you? He knew she was there. He'd

asked. He'd made damn sure before sitting out here where somebody might recognize him for the person he wasn't.

Then he saw. It wasn't the face he'd anticipated. The figure he should have wanted. He squinted, pulling the entire line of swaying, dipping women out of focus. He tried to settle different features on her. More delicate features, more high-boned, more…beautiful.

His Lilly hadn't lied. Whatever genes she'd possessed had, indeed, been too mangled to be beautiful. Her face was too flat, her nose a little too broad, her eyes a bit too wide, her body too stocky.

But as Ethan watched her with wide eyes, he saw the graceful flight of her fingers as they dipped and soared like birds in flight. He saw the special grace of her movements, music come to life in ankle and hip and bright, glowing smile. He heard again, even as she swayed in silence to the music, her bright, sparkling laugh as it had skipped over the water. And he knew that what she looked like didn't matter. Because while he had had his sight taken away, Ethan Campbell had learned what beauty really meant.

It wasn't high cheekbones and sleek lines. It wasn't even perfect lips and a straight nose. It was laughter and sense and the softest hands in the universe. It was the kind of compassion that lit a dark afternoon, the kind of humor that banished fear. It was the strength and wisdom and courage that gave his Lilly her magic.

And, he realized with amazement, he might never have known that if he hadn't been damn near blind.

He might, like every other shallow, selfish male on earth, have looked no further than that unique little face. The face some jerk on the television had likened to features whacked with a shovel.

Sitting there in a lawn chair, his drink forgotten, his

hands all but shaking with the sense of surprise, Ethan found himself stunned to his toes by the realization that he wouldn't want his Lilly Malama any other way.

He got to his feet long before the end of the set and walked into the side hall of the hotel where the dancers would exit. He watched from the side long enough to realize that something was missing from Lilly's movements. Something vital, as if the sun had been eclipsed. He hoped, like the shallow, selfish male he was, that it had to do with him. He prayed that she really did have a good reason for not calling back.

The first girl in line almost ran right into him. He grinned and apologized, and she almost fell on the floor.

"You're—"

"No, I'm not."

The second girl slammed into the first.

"Yes, you are. You're Lilly's *haole*."

Ethan grinned again. "Oh, well, in that case, yes. I am Lilly's *haole*."

By the time Lilly made it into the shadowy hallway, the rest of her line was standing in a clump just staring at Ethan. And Ethan was just staring at Lilly.

"What is this, a hula pileup?" she asked easily as she ran into her friends.

They parted like the Red Sea and stayed to watch.

Lilly didn't disappoint them.

Ethan had hoped she would be surprised. He hadn't counted on stunned.

"Oh, God..." She paled and swayed. He almost reached out a hand to her.

She reached out to him instead. Lilly, his toucher.

"Are you all right?" she asked. "Your eyes..."

Ethan was smiling just for her now. "You have the prettiest smile, Lilly. Did you know that?"

She pulled her hand away as if it had been scorched
"I..."

"Why didn't you call Noah back?"

She couldn't seem to answer. Ethan wished he could
ask everybody else to leave. Heck, he wished he could
tell them to go to hell.

"C'mon, everybody," one of them spoke up, as if hearing him. "We can catch the recap later." Then she
reached up and kissed Ethan's cheek. "It's about time you
showed up."

Before Ethan could think of an answer, they were all
off, chattering like bright birds. And he and Lilly were
left in a public hallway at the edge of the sunlight. Lilly's
eyes were over-bright, as if she were battling tears. She
looked as if she were steeling herself for something.
Something bad.

"Can we go somewhere and talk?" Ethan asked.

"I have another show."

"I think your friends will cover for you. Please, Lil.
There's so much I need to say."

She seemed to brace herself against something, and
then, as if it were too much, to wilt right before his eyes.

"Yes," she said, her voice small.

Ethan didn't give her a chance to change her mind.
Taking her by the hand, he pulled her along to the back
elevators the concierge had shown him so he could avoid
the public, who still saw him as Cameron Ross. And then
he swept Lilly up to the penthouse suite.

She didn't even seem to see the opulence of the room,
instead walking right out to the lanai. Ethan followed her,
his tired eyes taking in the expanse of Waikiki and Dia-
mond Head beyond.

"This is very nice," Lilly said, looking over the rail.

Ethan walked close enough behind her to smell her hair.

It provoked yet another smile, this one of deepest satisfaction. He'd dreamed of that smell through two hospitals and a solid month of Ellen's harangues. He'd hung on to that fragile bit of magic like a talisman through the worst.

"It may not be Molokai," he countered, his hands in fists to keep them away from her, "but it's not bad."

She turned on him, her eyes searching and worried. "Are you really okay? It hasn't been that long, Ethan. I mean…"

He did reach out then, catching her hands like startled birds and stilling them. "I'm fine, Lilly. I promise." He tried grinning. "I don't even need my glasses anymore. Not a bad deal, huh?"

She didn't pull free, but she distanced herself nonetheless, her head down, her body tense against injury. It was Ethan who felt it, though, as if he had some of that magic even Noah had recognized. He was so afraid, suddenly.

"Why did you just disappear?" he asked.

She seemed to lift her answer on tired shoulders. "I didn't disappear. I went home."

"And not one of your myriad family or friends let any of us near you. That's why I had to blindside you at the pool today."

Lilly pulled away and reached behind her to wrap her hands around the rail, as if that could keep her away from him. "I'm sorry," she said, as if she couldn't help it. "I'm so sorry."

"Because you couldn't face Ellen?" He grinned again. "Hell, Lilly, I've known her for ten years, and *I* couldn't face her."

Lilly seemed to stop breathing altogether. "Do you remember now?" she asked quietly. "Do you remember everything?"

Ethan nodded. "It came back like a movie with the reels out of order, but yes, Lilly. I remember it all."

She nodded, wide-eyed and still. "Which means you remember that Ellen is your wife."

Ethan grimaced. He should have known. They'd all been so distracted those first few days, nobody had kept a watch on Ellen. And Ellen, as ever, had been desperate for attention.

"My ex-wife," he said gently, stepping forward again.

She backed even farther against the rail. "Ex-wife or future ex-wife?"

Ethan smiled and closed the distance. He let her keep her hands free. Instead, he reached out to winnow one hand through the heavy silk of her hair where it lifted off her soft shoulder. "You know, we could have avoided all this if you'd just talked to Noah like he wanted. He had a feeling you'd run afoul of Ellen at the hospital. It was the only reason he could think of that you wouldn't come back. I told him that my Lilly Malama wouldn't be that kind of coward."

She straightened, and for the first time Ethan saw how hot the spark of outrage could burn in those midnight eyes. "So, you consider it cowardly not to push myself in the face of your wife? Exactly what was I supposed to say, Ethan? 'Excuse me, ma'am, I have more claim on him than you. After all, we've been bumping boots up on a hill on Molokai for the last twenty-four hours straight.'"

He touched the tear that had escaped from incredibly long eyelashes. "You didn't stay around to find out for sure. Why, Lilly?"

"Why?" In that one syllable of outrage, Ethan bet he could imagine what her Tutu Mary was like. Hell, he bet he could recognize Pele if she walked up the street. The heck with the earth, this woman was molten to the core.

and sore and battered as his body was, it responded far too predictably.

"Why?" she repeated half a tone up. "Because I looked enough of an idiot on national television without waiting around at the edges of the crowd hoping you'd notice me. Hoping you'd…you'd…" Tears fell faster, catching her breath and tightening her shoulders and hands. She let loose of the rail finally, but her hands were bunched at her sides, as if she had to physically fight the pain.

So Ethan fought any way he could. "I woke up and you weren't there, Lilly. You saved me with your *mana* and your soft hands, and you didn't even stay around to ease my way back." He reached out again to that impossibly taut face and reacquainted himself with the petal-soft feel of it. "I thought you didn't care if I lived or died."

Like a key to her emotions, his words unlocked the sobs. And Ethan, who had survived because of this woman's gentle strength, was able to hold her up instead. Hold her together, hold her close to his heart, where she'd taken up permanent residence.

"Don't you understand, Lilly?" he demanded, his cheek against her hair, his arms around her, his heart sore for her. "I love you. I love *you*."

"You couldn't possibly know," she argued, even with her own arms around him. "I couldn't take the chance—"

Ethan tipped her face up to him and slid off his sunglasses. He waited through her stricken gasp at the sight of the scars that still marred his once-classic features. And then, bending down, he kissed her. Softly. Gently. Thoroughly.

"You couldn't take the chance I was going to be a shallow bastard who couldn't love you if you didn't look like your sister the famous weather forecaster," he whispered just to her.

She shut her eyes, her cheeks flushed with shame. "Yes."

"Then I guess I have more to thank you for than just saving my pitiful, accident-prone life, don't I, Lilly? Because you single-handedly reminded me of something I've been forced to live with my whole life. The preconception people have of others just because of how they look. The press was stunned when Noah won his Oscar, because he was a pretty boy. I constantly surprise business associates, because they don't think I have a brain in my head. Well, I guess turnabout is fair play, Lilly. You gave me the chance to remember just what beauty is all about. And you, Lilly Malama, daughter of Molokai, are the most beautiful woman I've ever had the great privilege to know."

Ethan wanted to laugh at the expression on Lilly's face. Disbelief, wonder, fear. He wanted to sing at the thought that it was Lilly's own insecurities that had kept her away.

"I may not be Cameron Ross, Lilly," he said. "But I'm not a bad guy, either. And I really have been divorced for four years. I just had to settle for Ellen continuing in the business as part of a settlement I wanted very badly at the time. And, having met Ellen, you can imagine how well she handled the whole setup. You can ask Noah and Dulcy, if you're not sure. Want me to call them?"

Lilly's grin seemed to surprise her. "No. They're busy enough with the baby."

Ethan nodded, dropping a kiss on her forehead, inhaling the special scent of Lilly Malama that he would cherish to the day he cocked up his toes.

"So," he said, his voice as soft as the wind, "if you don't have any more objections, would you marry me?"

She still wasn't breathing. Ethan saw the emotions skim across those lustrous black eyes and thought he'd never seen anything so exquisite in his life.

"Oh, Ethan," she sighed, so softly he could hardly hear, her forehead pursed with distress. "How can I? You have a world to go back to. I have the islands I never want to leave."

And now, his biggest delight. "Funny you should mention that," he said. "We figured out why I decided to take a memory hike for so long. I've been dying to get away from the pressure for a long time. I just felt…"

"Responsible," she said, an impish dimple surprising him. "But what are you going to do, take up surfing?"

"I could if I wanted. I'm that filthy rich. But I'm still responsible for a lot of both Noah's and my investments. The wonderful thing is, though, we do, indeed, live in the computer age. I can do it from anywhere."

Her eyes grew impossibly large. "Anywhere?"

He ran a finger over her nose and thought that it was the most beautiful nose he'd ever seen. "Do you think we could go see your Tutu Mary and ask about bringing computers to the valley? I mean, you are going to own it."

This time he damn near had to hold her up.

"I also talked to Noah, who thought that it would be a really good idea to have a research librarian do some of the background research for the movies he does. He's going to be starting one on Mary, Queen of Scots. She was a Stuart, wasn't she?"

Lilly was shaking her head. "You're going too fast for me. How can I answer you? How can I let you isolate yourself in the mountains just because I want to? You *hate* the mountains. You told me. Noah told me. I don't want you miserable, Ethan."

Ethan took that intent little face in his hands and stilled her fears. "I hate the mountains of home because they were mean and poor and desperate. These mountains are different. These are...your mountains, Lilly. You've made them healing for me. Besides, we can work all that out later. Just answer my question. Will you marry me?"

She trembled like a wild bird caught in his hand. "We've only known each other a few days."

"I'll court you."

"You've never met my family."

"I don't care. I've met you. Please, Lilly. Save me again. Don't let me go home alone."

Tears again. Soft, silent tears that tracked down her sweet face like spring rain. "Well," she said, smiling right through them, "I'd have to take a life-saving course first."

Ethan laughed. "Snot."

"And explain to my family why I settled for a guy with a bent nose and railroad tracks on his cheek."

"It shows character."

She drew in a deep breath. "Our children would have Hawaiian names."

"One Hawaiian, one Scotch-Irish."

She nodded, then stiffened, as if only then realizing what she'd done. "You have the chance at any time to back out while we court, Ethan."

"So do you," he assured her, knowing that he, at least, wouldn't. "I snore, you know."

"Yes." Finally, that light sparking back in her eyes like a reclaimed sun. "I do."

"Does this mean you'll let me court you? Call on you with wilted flowers and bad poetry and bore you to death over dinner?"

"It means that if you still want to marry me in another two months, I'll be happy to marry you."

"Then I'd better get started, hadn't I?"

Bending his head to her, wrapping her tight in his arms, he did just that.

Epilogue

"Oh, Lilly, child," the old woman chortled, "you so funny. What, you think we no get new things down the mountain?"

Poised between her grandmother and the FAX machine she'd just installed in her new house, Lilly just smiled. "I didn't want to ruin the old voices up here, Tutu. I wasn't sure."

Tutu Mary patted the new equipment with a gnarled, misshapen hand. "You doin' good things, yeah? You use this for sharing the old ways. Nobody goin' be mad about that, foah suah."

Lilly smiled again, this time with belief. It only took one look at the powerful serenity of that strong-boned, exotic face, that thick waterfall of steel-gray hair, that regal posture, to know for certain that even the old ones wouldn't consider challenging her *tutu* when she made such a decision.

Slipping up behind Lilly, Ethan wrapped his arms around her waist. "I told you so. How d'you like it up in our nest, Tutu Mary?"

Lilly's grandmother lifted her sharp black eyes to the expanse of mountain, sky and water that could be seen beyond the near-endless windows of Lilly and Ethan's new house. Windows and wood, tucked into a nook in the Kokoa's valley a few hundred feet above Uncle Danny's cabin, nestled so neatly amid lush foliage that smelled of ginger and frangipani that most days the only evidence of its existence was the glint of sky against glass.

Ethan had kept his promise. He'd spent an obscene amount of money to put as much of the valley as he could into the Kokoa name, so that for all the generations to come, the Kokoas would have a home here in the island that had given them birth. He had brought Lilly home, and then he had helped her transform that home into something even more special. The ghosts she heard on the mountain no longer frightened her. The old ways called more gently, their responsibility lying more gently on Lilly's shoulders.

Because now she had someone to help share the load. Not that Ethan did any of her work. Not that he tramped up to the *heiau* along with her, where she and Tutu Mary had begun to catalogue the old healing plants for the University of Hawaii, or helped in the hula school where she taught little boys and girls the grace and dignity of their heritage. He spent his days managing his and Noah's empire from the den down the hall, where he could see that beach he so loved. Often he flew off to the mainland alone and returned anxious for his mountain. And always he brought back with him a peace and joy and sense of wholeness Lilly never should have found with someone not born in these islands.

"His island's not that different," Tutu Mary had said to her all those months ago when Lilly had asked her blessing. "His *mana* just as strong. Those old earth gods of his Celtic ancestors just like yours, little Lilly."

Now, as the three of them stood looking out upon what Ethan had brought them, Tutu Mary nodded, patted at Ethan's arm with grandmotherly hands, closed her eyes a moment in blessing, a quick sparkle of tears betraying the strength of her emotion.

"You do good, my new grandson. You do good."

The three of them stood a moment longer, soaking in the sight, until a spatter of footsteps announced guests. Ethan swung around just in time to scoop a little tow-headed toddler into his arms.

"There's my favorite godson," he sang, digging his face into the little boy's neck until he got a waterfall of giggles. "Where's everybody else?"

"Here," Dulcy called, one arm around her daughter, Hannah, a thin, bright, prepubescent version of herself, the other around a tan and relaxed Noah. "Uncle Danny just dropped us off. Boy, you really have to want to get here, don't you?"

Ethan and Lilly smiled with identical, secret smiles. "That's the idea. How do you like it?"

The redheaded girl walked right up to the old woman who bore the terrible scars of leprosy and hugged her. "This is your place, isn't it? You're Tutu Mary."

Tutu Mary patted away, eyes bright, face wreathed in a smile that had only hesitated a moment for Hannah's reaction. "Ah, you the symphony conductor, yeah?"

Hannah giggled. "Symphony composer. Can I compose something for here?"

"For now," Lilly's *tutu* corrected with another pat to that milky-soft cheek. "For all of you."

"All of us," Lilly corrected.

The rest of her family would join them all for the luau later in the day to celebrate their homecoming. There would be food and music and the hypnotic pull of the hula high up on the mountain. And all because of the man who had seen past Lilly's face into her heart. The man who said he recognized beauty because he'd known better than to try to see it. The man who had ignited Lilly's magic and sown his own, here, six thousand miles from the hard, beautiful hills where he'd been born.

Lilly stood here at the edge of her world, her arms around her husband, and knew that it could only get better. Lilly, the practical girl, the pragmatic woman, was gone. In her place was magical Lilly, and Ethan had been the one to perform the transformation.

"Beautiful child," Tutu Mary was saying, one arm around Hannah, one wrist against Ethan McCann's soft, plump face. "Beautiful life. It is good *mana*. Good men."

Suddenly the bright old eyes swung over to Lilly. "Powerful *mana*," she corrected herself, awe in that soft, ravelly voice. Then she smiled and touched Lilly's cheek. "A great *kahuna* comes," she whispered, and Lilly saw fresh tears. "A child who has much *mana*. Who weaves the magic of two places."

Lilly didn't say anything. Ethan looked at the two children gathered between them. "The symphony composer or the terror?" he asked.

But Tutu Mary was looking only at Lilly. "Neither," she said in her old voice, the one that echoed with centuries of power and prescience. "Here," she said, and laid that ravaged hand against Lilly's belly. Another smile. Another pat. "Here."

And Lilly, because she'd been given the gift of Ethan's

love, could smile back into her grandmother's eyes with perfect serenity. "I know."

Ethan stiffened, his mouth opened.

Lilly smiled up at him, at this man who might, finally, in another few months, begin to comprehend what he had wrought in her life.

"Her name will be Mary Malama Campbell," Lilly told them all, her new family and her old family, the one who came before and the ones who would come after, "and she will have the healing hands of her great grandmother and the magnificent heart of her father."

"And the unspeakable beauty of her mother," Ethan said, pulling her into his arms.

Lilly saw it then, there in his eyes. She saw the man, the power of a magic man. She saw herself the way he saw her, and knew that that was the way she was. She knew she was home, because she saw herself in his eyes. And she knew she never had to leave her mountain again.

* * * * *

If you enjoyed what you just read,
then we've got an offer you can't resist!

Take 2 bestselling
love stories FREE!
Plus get a FREE surprise gift!

Clip this page and mail it to Silhouette Reader Service™

IN U.S.A.
3010 Walden Ave.
P.O. Box 1867
Buffalo, N.Y. 14240-1867

IN CANADA
P.O. Box 609
Fort Erie, Ontario
L2A 5X3

YES! Please send me 2 free Silhouette Desire® novels and my free surprise
gift. Then send me 6 brand-new novels every month, which I will receive
months before they're available in stores. In the U.S.A., bill me at the bargain
price of $3.12 plus 25¢ delivery per book and applicable sales tax, if any*. In
Canada, bill me at the bargain price of $3.49 plus 25¢ delivery per book and
applicable taxes**. That's the complete price and a savings of over 10% off the
cover prices—what a great deal! I understand that accepting the 2 free books
and gift places me under no obligation ever to buy any books. I can always
return a shipment and cancel at any time. Even if I never buy another book from
Silhouette, the 2 free books and gift are mine to keep forever. So why not take
us up on our invitation. You'll be glad you did!

225 SEN CNFA
326 SEN CNFC

Name	(PLEASE PRINT)	
Address	Apt.#	
City	State/Prov.	Zip/Postal Code

* Terms and prices subject to change without notice. Sales tax applicable in N.Y.
** Canadian residents will be charged applicable provincial taxes and GST.
   All orders subject to approval. Offer limited to one per household.
   ® are registered trademarks of Harlequin Enterprises Limited.

DES99   ©1998 Harlequin Enterprises Limited

SILHOUETTE®

Desire

continues the captivating series from
bestselling author **Maureen Child**

BACHELOR
BATTALION

*Defending their country is their duty;
love and marriage is their reward!*

December 1999: **MARINE UNDER THE MISTLETOE
(SD#1258)**

took only one look for Marie Santini to fall head over heels for
arine sergeant Davis Garvey. But Davis didn't know if he was
apable of loving anyone. Could a Christmas miracle show him the
ue meaning of love?

**Start celebrating Silhouette's 20th anniversary
with these 4 special titles by
New York Times bestselling authors**

Fire and Rain
by Elizabeth Lowell

King of the Castle
by Heather Graham Pozzessere

State Secrets
by Linda Lael Miller

Paint Me Rainbows
by Fern Michaels

On sale in December 1999

Plus, a special free book offer inside each title

Available at your favorite retail outlet

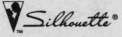

Visit us at www.romance.net

PSNYT